BROKER'S OPEN

A Real Estate Murder Mystery
In Duluth, Minnesota

LARRY STOLLER

BETTER BOOKS BUREAU
Bloomington, Minnesota

Printed in the United States of America
Published by Better Books Bureau
Bloomington, Minnesota
www.betterbooksbureau.bizland.com
betterbooksbureau@bizland.com

Library of Congress Catalog Card Number: 00-193268

ISBN 0-9707111-0-7

FIRST EDITION April, 2001

Cover art by Carole Booth, St. Paul, MN
Cover design by Lori Gnahn, Sartell, MN

For Flora, Harry, Helene, and Heather

Broker's Open author LARRY STOLLER delivers a
powerful, exciting, humorous, and touching tale
of murder, mystery, life, love, friendship, and
the pursuit of real estate on the shores of
Lake Superior in Duluth, Minnesota.

Larry Stoller is an accountant and real estate
broker in the Twin Cities in Minnesota.
Born and raised in Brooklyn, New
York, Stoller currently resides in
Bloomington, Minnesota with
his wife and daughter.

1

It is a cold, gray, first Tuesday in December in Duluth. With the disappearance of sunlight, things look dark and dreary. It feels as though evil forces that were contrary to nature had decided to shut out the sun. These forces built a thick ceiling of cement-like clouds that covered the sky. Then they painted the clouds a dark, dismal gray. It is very depressing, and it makes me feel sad and lonely. But I shouldn't feel that way today. In fact, there is no reason for me to feel sad and lonely today. For today, Sherry Stensgard, a top agent from our real estate office, is holding a broker's open house at my new and prestigious listing at Bedford House. That should make me feel happy. It should be a great day!

Besides, it's December, the biggest holiday month of the year. "Happy Holidays," "Merry Christmas," "Joy to the World," and all that sort of thing. But the truth of the matter is that December can be a very melancholy and miserable month. I know that from my days as a police detective in Washington, D.C. Thinking about those days made me remember that a lot of crime took place during the month of December. I also remember reading about depression in some very thick textbooks when I was studying psychology back in college. Some of those references indicated that December was a tough month to get through, and that it was very depressing for many. The more I think about it, the more I feel that today would be a good day to be with family or friends. Or with someone you loved, or at least liked. But not alone. No, it is already a lonely kind of day. To be alone would only make it worse, much worse.

Traditionally, Tuesdays are always the best days for broker's open houses. Not Mondays. Mondays are used for completing all the weekend sales and purchases. Tie up all the loose ends from the big weekend deals, and get the new week's schedule squared away. Not Wednesdays or Thursdays. These are the "production days," to be used for cold-calling, prospecting, listing appointments, market analyses, listing input, and whatever else it takes to obtain new business. Not Saturdays or Sundays. These are the traditional open house days, to showcase your sellers' homes. The weekends are also used to go house shopping with your prospective buyers. Both Saturdays and Sundays are very busy days in the real estate business. Not Fridays. Fridays are used for getting the weekend showings set up or for finalizing the past week's deals before the weekend hustle begins. Friday is also the day for rest and relaxation or for slacking off. Since returning to Duluth a few months ago, I've heard that you can pick up some good real estate tips or catch up on the latest real estate gossip Friday morning at the local golf course.

A 1 to 3 p.m. time frame will be ideal for my broker's open. Sherry will have some hot apple cider brewing and assorted muffins for the visiting brokers and realtors. That's the right stuff for a successful broker's open. That and an elegant expensive house, that's the ticket. And Bedford House fits the ticket perfectly. Who knows, maybe one of these brokers already has a buyer for this beauty. That would be great, a fast sale, a quick closing, and no inventory to keep around. Yes, that'd be great, but if not, I'll find a buyer. It shouldn't be too difficult to sell a $1.2 million mansion that sits atop a two-acre wooded lot overlooking Lake Superior.

A trip through Duluth is like taking a journey through time. It's 1983, but elegant homes and mansions from an earlier era still stand proud and prominent on many of the city's streets. Many of the great houses of Duluth were built between 1890 and 1925. These magnificent mansions and historic homes expressed the great wealth that was created during the business booms in mining, shipping, and lumber that took place in Duluth during the late 1800's and early 1900's.

The mansion on London Road known as Bedford House is a twenty-six-room castle-like structure that was built along the rocky shore of Lake Superior. Bedford boasts stunning views of the lake from many rooms through massive stone arches and beautiful leaded glass windows.

The design of the house is a mix of English Renaissance and Tudor styles of architecture, and it is built of cream-colored rubble stone and half-timbers with sloping slate roofs and towering chimneys reaching up to the tallest trees. The exterior of the house resembles a noble medieval castle set back in a forest of large mature pines, oaks, and evergreens. The entryway is impressive and leads into a huge foyer of open architecture supported by massive stone columns and wood beams surrounded by a sea of solid rich teak floors. The different types of stone supports and archways, intermingled with rich textures of earthen-tone oak and pine paneling, produce an image of medieval times and foster feelings of simplicity and charm of years gone by.

The inside of the home was altered to serve the needs of modern day living while preserving the beauty, charm, and elegance of times past. The combination of wood tones, earth-colored tile, and stone fireplaces in many of the major rooms adds feelings of warmth and comfort that are unmatched in similar period homes. There is beautiful pine paneling with carefully carved detail from England and Scotland. Elegant brushed brass chandeliers and brilliant white crystal lighting extend from high ceilings which are typical of the age and the style of English architecture. Many of the rooms offer panoramic views of Lake Superior; from others, picturesque gardens and a variety of towering, mature, and majestic trees can be seen.

The warmth and glow from the mansion's brick and marble wood-burning fireplace in the living room, overlooking the big lake, would be very inviting. Especially on a cold, gray, dreary day like today.

And the commission on this house, if some other agent brings in the buyer, will be 6 percent. That comes to $72,000 and my share would be 3 percent, $36,000. If I bring in the buyer, I'll get 5 percent, which comes to $60,000. And I'm a heck of a hogger from way back. "Stone the hogger." I've always had good luck in finding buyers for my own listings. Just thinking about these numbers makes me feel warm inside, even without the fireplace burning brightly. That's what I'll work on today, finding the right buyer for this exceptional home, while Sherry Stensgard from our office holds this broker's open for me.

She practically begged me to let her hold the open, and that's fine. She was very excited about doing the broker's open on this magnificent mansion. I walked her through the place the day before, so she'd know the routine, and be familiar with all the nooks and crannies in the big house. Well, at least most of the nooks and crannies. I'm sure there are some that have yet to be discovered. She really got into this house. She's a successful agent who loves her work, and I could see how easy it would be for any home owner to say to her, "I'd like you to sell my house." I asked her if I should stop by during the open. She told me, sure, if I wanted to, but that I didn't have to be there and that I didn't have to worry. I was comfortable with her and there was no reason for me to be there. I could work on making some calls and maybe getting this hunk of a home sold before the day was over.

I should have been there though. Every day I think, if only I'd been there. There were plenty of reasons for me to be there, too. I could have helped open up the house, turn the lights on in all the rooms, and get things set up. With it being so cold outside, I could have got a fire going in one of the fireplaces. Or I could have stayed around until the first couple of visitors showed up, and then left, just to make sure that everything was okay. Better yet, I could have stayed there for the entire three hours. We could have done the open house together. With a "twenty-six-room castle," two doing the open would have been better than one. And then I could have helped her close up the house also. I really should have been there. God, can't we just change one small part of that day? Could you just let me be there instead of her? God, I wish I'd been there!

But I was not there. I was at All Duluth Realty.

And at 1:30 p.m. I received a call from Duluth

BROKER'S OPEN

Detective Lieutenant June Brown. Detective Brown said that Sherry Stensgard was murdered at Bedford House. Could I come by right away to identify the body?

2

A s I drove up the hill to Bedford House, I couldn't help feeling agitated and uneasy. I also felt confused and disconnected, thinking to myself, "How could something like this happen." These feelings stayed with me, like uninvited guests who would not leave. At the top of the hill, a uniformed officer waved me to stop and asked my business. I indicated that Detective Brown had called me to come over to identify the body. He looked at my driver's license, took down my name, and pointed to a place where cars were parked, and then forgot about me.

There was crime scene tape strung across the drive and in between some of the trees. I walked up to the door, turned the knob gently, pushed, and entered. Inside, there were busy people, and the unmistakable buzz of police business had transformed the mansion into something very different from what it had been yesterday when Sherry and I walked through it and talked about it. Yesterday it had been magical, mystical, and medieval. Today it could have passed as a meeting place for a police convention. I took a few steps forward and was stopped by a triple extra large suit and a huge paw of a hand in my face that blocked out everything else that was in front of me. "How'd you get in here? What are you doing here?" The policeman's voice from behind the paw sounded gruff and intimidating to me. I repeated what I'd said to the other officer. "And who are you?" he barked.

"I'm Larry Stone. Sherry Stensgard and I worked together at All Duluth Realty." I followed the detective. He looked like a huge bulldog in an extra large suit. We walked through the foyer to the living room, where he reported to his superior that a Larry Stone was here to identify the body. A petite black female, Detective Lieutenant June Brown, stood in front of me and introduced herself, dismissed the suit, and led me into the living room. The living room, like the rest of the house, was now decorated with strips of yellow tape accented by black lettering that defined the scene of the murder.

There lay Sherry Stensgard, her face a mask of surprise and sadness, a look of disbelief and incomprehension, and her body maimed and motionless, with a "For Sale" sign stuck inside her, surrounded by a stream of crusting red blood. I stared at her face, then looked away in sadness and disgust. During the ten years that I'd been on the force, I'd seen this hundreds of times. Although I had become hardened to the sights of death, the innocent faces were still hard to erase. So now, Sherry's face kept flashing in front of my eyes and inside my head. Lieutenant Brown indicated that Sherry had been strangled, hit on the head, and then this "For Sale" sign had been plunged into her stomach, creating a pool of blood. The word "NOT" was penned in blood on the sign just before the words "For Sale."

"It's horrible and sickening that someone would do this," she added. "I know it's not easy for you to look at her, but I need you to confirm her identification as Sherry Stensgard."

"Yes, it's Sherry Stensgard. I mean it was Sherry Stensgard." I didn't know what to think or what to say. I looked into Detective Brown's eyes and saw compassion and then anger. In a low voice and very slowly I said, "Why this? Why Sherry?"

"I'm sorry, Mr. Stone, but I'll need to ask you some questions now. Then some more later. Be in my office tomorrow morning at nine. Here's my card."

She continued, "Let's walk over here a bit. Now, I need to know what was going on here today, Mr. Stone, or what was supposed to go on here today?"

"It was a broker's open, Lieutenant, from one to three."

"A what?"

"A broker's open. It's like an open house that's advertised in the newspaper so that prospective buyers could come to look it over, see if they like it, and see if they want to buy it. However, since this was a broker's open, only real estate brokers and agents were invited for a personal and private preview of the home in case they had any prospective buyers."

"I see. But when I called All Duluth Realty, they said this was your house, so what was she doing here?"

"They meant my listing, Lieutenant, not my house. I was hired by the owners to sell the house, and I was going to do this broker's open, but Sherry asked me, persuaded me to let her hold the open. So I went through the house with her yesterday so that she'd be familiar with it, so that she could hold it open today. So that she would know all about it, its features and its history." I stopped talking and looked around. Everything seemed to be in slow motion. Slowly I said, "I can't believe this happened."

After another moment of reflection, I commented, "Sherry was such a good person. Always happy and helpful. A smile on her face, and a smile in her voice. Everybody liked her." I was looking at Detective June Brown, then past her, gazing at the tired clouds that covered the sky. I felt stuck somewhere between a dismal daydream and a horrible nightmare.

Detective Brown snapped me out of it. She took my arm and sat me down on a nearby sofa. "Mr. Stone, are you okay?"

"Oh, yes, okay. I'm okay."

"Don't forget. Tomorrow morning at nine. My office. Police Headquarters."

"Yes, I know. I have your card. I'll be there."

3

There was just enough time to drop by the office to see if I had any messages before meeting with Detective June Brown. As I opened the office door, I noticed a plain white envelope resting on the carpet inside the office. I picked it up and saw that it was addressed to me. I opened it and read what was written on the paper inside—"LEAVE JEW. DON'T SELL HERE. OR WORSE WILL HAPPEN." The words grabbed me, shook me, and then held me in a vise-like grip. All I could do was keep staring at the words, my eyes glued to the paper, and my body immobile. When my brain released my body, I looked away, and located a cellophane pouch on a desk nearby. I carefully put the paper and envelope into the plastic pouch, sealed it, and put it in my jacket pocket. I also tried to shake off some troublesome feelings. I was able to get rid of *threatened* and *alienated*, but *helpless* and *defiled* stayed with me. And then *anger* joined them.

As I closed the door and started walking toward my car, my anger grew intense and pulsated wildly within me. I wanted to lash out at someone or something, but at whom or what I did not know. I took a number of deep breaths before getting into the car, and then a few more once I was inside the car. I felt inside my pocket to make sure the pouch was still there. I confirmed that it still was, and then drove to Duluth Police Headquarters for my meeting with Detective Brown.

Police Detective Lieutenant June Brown is diminutive in size but not in shape, style, or presence. With two large male detectives in the room with her, all 5'1" of her is awesome and totally in control.

"Your name's Larry Stone, and you're a real estate agent at All Duluth Realty."

"Actually I'm a broker-owner and one of the partners there."

"Okay, partner, and you've only been back in Duluth for what, about two months now?"

I thought I detected some sarcasm, but I couldn't be sure. I answered her question, "Yes, about two months."

"And in these two months, you list this big old house overlooking the lake, have an open house, and one of your agents gets brutally murdered there about fifteen minutes after she arrives?" I nodded at the detective, thinking this must be some kind of responsibility for a woman, and even more for a black woman. Especially a black woman in Duluth. I hadn't seen a lot of color in Duluth, and here in the Duluth Police Precinct the dominant color is white and the gender male. "This is a terrible murder, the way it was done, and the staging afterwards. You saw that house sign stuck inside her and the word 'NOT' written in blood?"

"Yes, I did."

"Any ideas about what's going on here, Mr. Stone? Eight weeks in Duluth and this. I don't remember having seen anything like this here in Duluth. Such a disgusting and hateful murder."

"I stopped in at my office this morning before coming here, Lieutenant, and this note was under the office door, addressed to me," I said angrily.

"Let's see it!" I handed it to her. She read out loud, "LEAVE JEW. DON'T SELL HERE. OR WORSE WILL HAPPEN." She gasped, and then paused in thought. "Such hatred directed at you. Who wants you to leave Duluth? Who hates you that much to do such a thing? Who? Any ideas, Mr. Stone? A rival realtor, an old enemy, a jealous boyfriend, a jealous husband, an ex-lover, a new enemy? Why? Someone who didn't want you to sell that house, someone who didn't want anyone to sell that house? What's this all about?"

I said I didn't know. "Well, think about it, Mr. Stone. Think hard. There's someone out there who hates you insanely. He doesn't want you around, and from the looks of it, he'll do anything to get rid of you. Did you do anything over the past eight weeks that would cause this to happen?"

"Well, I listed this mansion, and I had planned to spend a lot of time getting it sold. I wish I hadn't listed it," I said ruefully.

"Yes, I hear you. Okay, here is what I need for you to do. For the rest of the day think about why this happened. Make a list for me of all the contacts you've made since your return to Duluth. Who you've spoken to. Who you've been with. I want a diary of your past eight weeks in Duluth. I also want to know who you had contacted just before you got here, and any past contacts you can recall as well. I know you lived here and went to school here many years ago. Did you have any high school enemies, college enemies, arguments, fights, bad incidents, anything like that? What did you do when you used to live here? Include whatever you can think of that might help. We're dusting the house, going over every inch of it, but with a big house like that, it's going to take a while. Hopefully we'll come up with something, but my guy from the lab tells me it's pretty clean so far. A disgusting dirty killing done cleanly." She turned on her heels and called out, "Get me that list today. As soon as you can."

"Okay, Lieutenant, I'll get it to you today."

Before I left, one of the detectives, the extra large one with a face full of cascading jowls, asked me where I'd been all morning yesterday. I told him, "At the office."

He said, "Which office?"

I said, "All Duluth Realty." He asked if anyone could confirm that. I looked at him and then past him and said, "Yes." He then asked me what my relationship was with Ms. Stensgard. That question and the way he asked it disturbed me. I stared at him for a moment before replying. I then said, "We were co-workers. She was a second year agent. I am a broker-owner and firm partner."

He then said with a sly look in his eyes, "She's some piece of ass. Were you getting any?"

I locked eyes with him and told him he was out of line, and maybe someone should wash his fat filthy mouth out with soap. He jumped up and came toward me. "Why, you goddamn little shit." Just as he got the "shit" out of his mouth, Detective June Brown flung herself in front of him and shoved him back three feet. She then ordered in a loud and commanding voice, *"Out of here, now!"* To the other suit she said, *"Get him out of here. Cool him off."* She pointed a finger at jowl face and said, *"Be in my office in an hour."*

When they were gone, she said, "I'm sorry about that, Mr. Stone." She was not used to apologizing for her detectives, but she did so in a straightforward manner.

I felt sorry that she had to work with that fat jerk. I said, "Larry's fine, and it's okay."

"No, it's not okay, Larry. It was disgusting and distasteful. I'll chew him up good for that outburst. I get sick and tired of this male macho-crap, and when I get done with him, he'll be one sorrowful-ass, if you know what I mean." Detective Brown was very angry. She was in control but she was fuming.

"Yes, I think I know what you mean," I said matter-of-factly.

"Now, Larry," she asked. "Were you intimate with the deceased? Or did you try to be?"

I looked into her eyes and I replied, "No, June, I mean Lieutenant."

Her voice softened as she said, "We're alone, June's fine."

I finished what I had wanted to say. "I was not intimate with her, and I did not try to be. I only knew her for a couple of months."

"What was she like, Larry? Could you tell me anything about her?"

"Sherry was a beautiful person, June. She was very kind, caring, and concerned. Very mature for a twenty-seven-year-old. She talked to everyone in the office and made them feel good about themselves. Everybody liked her. She was like a breath of fresh air in the office. She was also very pretty, naturally pretty. But even if I had romantic thoughts or inclinations, we worked in the same office. I'm not going to get involved with someone I work with."

"Really, Larry, you wouldn't see someone who worked in the same office?" she questioned invitingly.

"No, June, I wouldn't. Even if I wanted to. I'd wait until we weren't working in the same office," I said with conviction.

"Ah, you're an old-fashioned type, Larry. That's nice. I'll see you later with that list."

4

I was born in Brooklyn, New York in 1944, and I lived there for fourteen years before moving to Minnesota. As an adolescent New Yorker, I had no idea where Minnesota was on the map, let alone Duluth, Minnesota. Yet at fourteen, I moved from Brooklyn to Duluth. It appeared that Duluth was my destiny. After the car accident in the Catskills, I was parentless in Brooklyn. No one really wanted a skinny, freckled, sometimes outspoken boy who was very sad, sensitive, sentimental, and who was approaching manhood sooner than others of his age. Except the Johnson family from Duluth. They wanted me. I suppose one of my dad's brothers or my mom's sister would have taken me in, but the Johnsons were there for me, and my being a part of their family made a lot of sense and felt right to me. Not just right, but good and right. The first time I met them, at my parents' funeral, it felt good being with them. After reading the letters that my mom and Melanie Johnson had sent back and forth to each other, it felt right being with them also. I had a good life in Brooklyn, but that part of my life was over. My new life would be with the Johnsons, in Duluth.

5

I was an only child and my parents were also my best friends. I never had to compete for their affection and they were always there when I needed them. Life was easy back then, and growing up in Brooklyn left me with a lot of good memories. My mom, dad, and I lived in a one-bedroom apartment, on the fourth floor of a well-kept brick building with no elevator. It was located between Brighton Beach and Coney Island, a block or two from the ocean. In the winter, you could see the boardwalk and the ocean through the leafless trees in the park across the street. It was a great place to live. It might have been nice to own a house, but we couldn't afford one, so we rented. Or maybe we didn't think we could afford one, or we just didn't know. Real estate education back then was not that aggressive, nor that readily available. Potential clients were not sought after, nor were they shown home ownership versus home renting comparisons, indicating that home ownership could cost the same as or less than renting. Back then, subjects such as FHA mortgages, down payments, first time homebuyer assistance, interest rates, monthly payments, and tax-savings were the last things discussed at the dinner table, if they were discussed at all.

My family was very loving. They may not have said that they loved me a lot, but I knew that they did. And it made me feel good. Very good. My dad was a musician, a drummer. My mom was a secretary. We never had a lot of money, but the bills were always paid. We never went hungry. We went out to eat once in a while, and the three of us went on some pretty nice vacations. Like to Long Island or the Catskills in upstate New York. Since my dad was never on a plane, and never intended to be, our "lavish" vacations were limited by how far we could drive and how much time we had to stay. The Catskills vacations were great. During the summers, my father had a job as a musician at one of the "not so famous" Catskills hotels. In fact, he was the leader of the band. We would be given a room close to the clubhouse, where the band used to play on Friday and Saturday nights. Actually, it was in the attic of the clubhouse. I used to fall asleep each night listening to the music from my dad's band. I became a devoted fan of the old standards, and I knew many tunes and the words to many songs by heart, especially the Al Jolson songs. I knew all of them, as they were my father's favorites. The band would play and my dad would lightly tap or brush the drums and sing, and many people thought he sounded like Al Jolson himself. My dad's big hit was "April Showers." The hotel guests would dance or just sit and listen. Many times they would join in. Sometimes I would also. Most of the time, I would sing when I was alone, or with my parents. They were the summer lullabies that sent me off to sleep every Friday and Saturday night. Once in a great while, my mom would sing. Her rendition of "Under a Blanket of Blue" was beautiful. I have no recording of it, but I can hear it in my head whenever I want to. On weekdays, I had plenty of records, and some tape recordings of my dad's music that I could listen to. Now and then, the band would play on Sunday afternoons. Then my dad and the rest of the musicians would drive to Manhattan to work their regular jobs. Dad was a printer from Monday through Thursday and a musician on the weekends. My mom and I would stay at the hotel during the week, and my dad would join us every weekend. My Catskills vacation started in July and ended sometime around Labor Day. What a wonderful and carefree life we had during the summer months.

When summer was over, our good life continued. We'd eat together, watch television together, see movies together, sing together, and talk together. It was wonderful, and I was so happy that sometimes I wanted to stop the clock and stay a kid forever. Yet at other times, I would think about getting older, going to college or work, and being away from my mom and dad. I also thought we would lose each other. I never shared this thought with them, but there were nights when I would envision that I would be gone or they would be gone, and we wouldn't be able to get together. On those nights I would wake up in the dark, feeling sad and lonely, and then cry myself back to sleep. It didn't happen that much, but when it did, I always kept it to myself. Those sad and lonely feelings would come to visit me when summer was over and when school started. But during the summer, those feelings were nowhere in sight, and I was happy most of the time. And it was still summer. And the summer time was the best!

6

On a sunny Saturday morning in August, my parents drove off to the market in the next town about fourteen miles away. I was playing with some other kids, when they told me they'd be back in an hour or two. But they drove off and never returned. Instead, the local sheriff arrived to tell me that my parents had been in an automobile accident, and that I needed to go with him right away. We arrived at the place of the accident and I saw my parents' car, but it looked different, like a toy car that was squashed in the front and back. It looked more like a big accordion than a car. There were police cars, fire engines, and an ambulance with its siren screaming speeding away from us. We followed the ambulance to the hospital. At the hospital I saw my parents. They looked so still and sad. Almost unreal. No smiles on their faces. They didn't see me. They would never see me again. They would never smile at me again. I remembered when I was younger I would see the way they looked at me and smiled at me, and I could always feel their love inside me. Even when I was at school, or away from them playing with my friends, I could always see their happy faces. They were always with me. I could not understand how they could leave me if they loved me so. But they did leave me. They didn't want to, but now they're gone. No more smiles, no more holding hands, no more their arms around me. No more their love.

7

The day before the funeral I visited my parents at the Pine Hill Funeral Home in Queens, New York. It was a chilly day for August, and there were many dirty white and dark gray clouds floating in the sky. No sun, just all these clouds with angry crinkled faces floating motionless above. They hovered overhead and made me feel that time had stopped. At the funeral home I saw my uncles Milt and Jack, my father's brothers, and my aunt Irene, my mother's only sister. And I saw my mom and dad lying peacefully next to each other inside separate dark wooden coffins. They didn't look angry and they didn't look sad. They didn't look like anything that I could remember. They looked like big dolls. They weren't smiling, and they didn't see me.

My uncles Milt and Jack and aunt Irene were looking at me. I looked at them. They asked if I was okay, and I said "No. This is not right. This is all wrong."

Jack, the oldest of the three, said, "It was a terrible accident, we all loved them, and we will all miss them."

I said, "That's true, but that's not what I mean. I mean that they should both be in the same coffin, together, and that they should be buried together. That's the way they would have wanted it." All three of them looked at my parents and then looked at me.

Jack said, "This is the way it's done. It was already set up this way, and it will be fine this way."

I looked at the three of them. My eyes locked onto theirs in a penetrating stare, and very loudly I said, *"No!"* And then very slowly and softly I explained, "They are my parents, and they've always been together in life, and they will now be together in death." No one said anything. I looked at my parents lovingly. Then I looked at their siblings in a way that they'd probably never been looked at before by a fourteen-year-old. It was an angry glare that was supplemented by disdain and defiance. It suggested that they dare not even think about disagreeing with what I said and with what I was about to say.

Then I found the funeral home director. I told him that I wanted one coffin for both of my parents, and that I intended to wait there until they were both lying side by side. He looked at my aunt and uncles. They slowly nodded their heads and said nothing. The funeral director looked at me and admitted that although a double coffin was seldom used, they had a few. He asked if I wanted to pick one out.

I responded, "Yes, I would," and the two of us walked away together to look at coffins. I looked at three and picked the one that was least dark, that looked most peaceful, and that felt the softest inside.

The funeral director said, "That's the best choice," and asked me to follow him. He asked if it would be okay for me to sit and wait while he and his assistants worked, and then look at my parents again.

I said, "Yes, that's what I would like to do." An hour later I viewed my parents' bodies again, lying together in one large coffin. Nothing changed, and everything changed. My parents were still dead, but they were now smiling, and I was sure that somehow they were seeing me. It was still wrong that they should be gone, but the way they looked now was right.

And that was the last time I saw them. My uncle Jack asked me if I wanted to spend the night at his home with his family. I thanked him, but I told him that I wanted to go home for a bit and that I would call later. My aunt said that I should be with someone, and my uncles agreed, but I told them I needed to be alone a bit and that I would call later. And that's the way it was.

I slept in my mom and dad's one-bedroom apartment alone that night. I kept the light on in my room, the living room, and tightly held on to a picture of my parents with me in the middle, their arms around me, their happy faces. I didn't get much sleep that night, and a number of times I woke up and went into their bedroom to look for them. But they weren't there. That night I cried more than I ever had before. I cried myself to sleep many times that night. In the morning, I awoke in my mom and dad's bed, with their picture in my hand. My mom and dad were smiling at me, holding me, and hugging me again. I knew how much they loved me and how much I would miss them. I felt very sad. My sadness stayed with me, like a heavy weight that was attached to my head and my heart. Now and then, it would lighten, as loving memories and happy thoughts briefly visited me from the past.

The phone rang. I thought I'd heard that ringing on and off throughout the night. But I had shut out the sound, and after a while the ringing became a melodic chiming that synchronized with my sleep. Or it had stopped altogether. But now it was a clear ringing, and I picked up the phone and said hello. It was my aunt Irene, and in a sobbing voice, she asked if I was all right. I replied that I was okay. Aunt Irene said that she would pick me up in about two hours to go to the funeral. I said that I would be ready.

Although I was now alone in the world, Mom, Dad, and I had been together again that night. We had said our last good-byes somewhere in the uneasy slumber of the night, somewhere between sleep, no sleep, sadness, memories, happy thoughts, and so many tears. Today would just be a funeral, a burial with one box to bury instead of two. That would be that. No more crying. There were no tears left.

8

On the day of the funeral, it was again unseasonably cool for August. Now there were many sad-looking clouds that sprinkled intermittent raindrops below. They darkened the sky and shut out the light, and everything looked dim and dismal. The sun had decided not to come out today. Very appropriate for a funeral, I thought. I had done my crying the night before, and now stood silent, listening to but not hearing words of consolation, as the large double coffin was lowered into the ground.

My dad's brothers and my mom's sister were there, along with their families. Also attending were a great-aunt, a great-uncle, and my parents' friends from the neighborhood and work. Two of my friends who lived in the same apartment building were there with their parents, and they looked sad and scared. There were also some people there whom I didn't know: one man and two women that I didn't recognize. I'd once been told that some people go to funerals even though they never knew the deceased. There was also what looked like a family of four, husband, wife, son, and daughter that I'd never seen before. They looked at me through sad eyes. The mother had tears in her eyes and sobbed quietly. The daughter, I would guess she was close to my age, or perhaps younger, wiped teardrops from her eyes. The son, who seemed to be a little older than I was, looked serious and somber. The dad's expression was one of compassion, caring, and understanding, as if he'd been through this before, and had seen and felt what I was seeing and feeling now.

All of the visitors walked by me, stopped, and tried to ease my pain by saying nice things to me, such as how bad they felt, or how much they would miss my parents. It felt comforting to have all these people here at this time. One of my little cousins was crying, and I heard her ask my aunt why I wasn't crying. My aunt told her that I had already cried so much before that there were no tears left inside me to cry now. I didn't know if she really knew how right she was. I had already done my crying.

After everyone had passed, the family of four came over to me. They looked very sad and slightly out of place. They stopped in front of me, and the woman spoke. She held my hand and spoke softly to me, "I'm Melanie Johnson. Your Aunt Irene called me. Your mom and I were the dearest of friends, and we spent a lot of time together, before I went off to Duluth to get married and start my family. We wrote many letters to each other. I put them together in a package. Here they are. I'd like you to have them. We both promised each other that we would be there for each other's children, if something ever happened to us and if our children ever needed us. We're here for you now if you need us." As she said that, the family of four formed a circle around me and enclosed me in a gentle and loving hug. They held me and hugged me with tears in their eyes and tenderness in their touch. I felt their sorrow and their caring deep inside me, and my eyes watered and I wept once more. The tears came and went very quickly. I felt safe, secure, and connected again. It felt good to cry quietly one last time.

9

The Johnsons adopted me, and I was on my way to Duluth in August of 1958. All the things I wanted from the apartment were packed: my clothes, a lot of photos, my birth certificate, my old report cards, some other personal papers, and a number of items that belonged to my mom and dad. There were my mom's jewelry, my dad's watches, and all the records and tape recordings of songs and music that were so much a part of our lives. I also took the stereo, the tape recorder, my hide-a-bed sofa, and an antique dresser for my clothes. The rest of the stuff, furniture, clothes, and things like that, my aunt and uncles said they would dispose of for me. There was a life insurance policy that I had never known about. A $50,000 check would be mailed to me in Duluth. There was also $17,000 in my parents' savings account. I wondered if we could have bought a house with it.

I wasn't happy about leaving Brooklyn. I suppose I could have stayed if I wanted to, but no one jumped up and down and made a big deal about me staying. I didn't think my aunt or uncles were particularly interested in having a skinny, freckled fourteen-year-old stay with them on a permanent basis, especially one who could be stubborn, say no, and glare at them the way I had done at the funeral home. Besides, after reading the letters that Mom and Melanie had sent to each other, I didn't want to stay in Brooklyn anymore. In the letters, Mom said that if anything ever happened to her and Dad, she wanted me to be with Melanie and her family. That was good enough for me.

I didn't know anyone in Duluth except for my new adoptive family, Ruby, Melanie, Randy, and Linda. I'd never had siblings, but if I were to have them, I'd want them to be like Randy and Linda. They shared everything with me, including their parents, and I felt comfortable being with them. I felt the same way about Ruby and Melanie. They treated me like they treated Randy and Linda. They had rules that were to be followed, very fair rules I thought. And they were always kind and loving. The Johnsons were Lutheran and went to church on a regular basis. I was Jewish, but I'd go with them anyway. The Lutheran pastor gave me a very warm welcome. He knew that I was of the Jewish faith, that I was a member of the Johnson family, and that I would continue to attend services. He shared that information with his congregation. I wished he hadn't. There weren't many Jews in Duluth, and Melanie and Ruby asked me how I felt about going to church with them. I said that it was okay, but that I wanted to stay in touch with my religion. I explained that I had had a bar mitzvah when I was thirteen, and that even though I was not "religious," I wanted it to always be a part of me. Melanie said she understood, and that she had copies of all of the bar mitzvah pictures that my mom had sent to her. Melanie introduced me to a rabbi in Duluth. I liked him right away, and I think he liked me. The plan was for me to visit the synagogue and congregation now and then, and to take part in the services.

It really bothered me that I didn't know anyone in Duluth. I'd probably meet people and get to know them at church, or maybe when I went to the synagogue. I was sure I'd meet kids and make friends when high school started. But for now, I felt very lonely, even though most everyone was friendly and nice.

10

Randy asked me to join him on a Saturday morning to play tackle football with some of the guys who would be going to East High School. He said it would be a good way to meet the guys before school started. I wasn't much of a football player, but I thought I might as well meet some of my future classmates, so Randy and I went to the park to play tackle football. There were about twenty-five of us there; no one wore helmets or any kind of protective gear. Randy explained how the teams were chosen—strictly by neighborhood. There were twelve guys from their neighborhood and thirteen from ours. Neighborhood against neighborhood. Ten players on the field from each team. That's it. Whoever the team captain was would decide who played and who stayed out. Since I was new, I stayed out in the beginning. But after about ten minutes I got the call to come in on defense. I was about 5'7" and weighed about 130 pounds. Football was not my game, and it never would be. But if it had been my game, I think I'd have been better on offense than on defense. I came in on defense as directed.

Their quarterback was a huge kid they called Big Howie. Big Howie was about 6'1" and must have weighed about 250 pounds. From where I stood, he looked like a giant Coca-Cola bottle, with round sloping shoulders and large arms and hands. He didn't look muscular, but I thought to myself, I wouldn't want to be tackled by him, or for that matter have to tackle him when he was running full steam ahead. I imagined it would be like bumping into a railroad train head on. I didn't think I'd have to worry too much about tackling him anyway, because the kid across from me on offense, who was getting ready to get into my face, was bigger and heavier than I was. He looked like a tough blocker, and I was pretty sure that it wouldn't be easy for me to get past him. Randy told me a little about Big Howie. He was the school bully, and he got into a lot of fights. He beat up other kids whom he didn't like, and it was rumored that he once pushed a teacher down a flight of stairs. Randy said that he once saw a fight between Big Howie and Chucky Padulowski. It was close, but at 5'6" and 220 pounds, Padulowski was faster and stronger and was hurting Big Howie more than Big Howie was hurting him. If some firemen, who happened to be riding by, hadn't separated the two, Chucky probably would have kicked Big Howie's butt. Randy pointed out Chucky Padulowski to me. Thank God he was on our team.

On the first play, Big Howie kept the ball and ran for about nine yards, as two of our guys hit him from the front and I hit him from the side and between the three of us, he went down. On the second play, Big Howie looked at me and said loudly enough for everyone to hear, "Look, they got a goddamn Jew on their team."

Without even thinking, I shot back, "I'd rather be a Jew than a fat, ugly, stupid shithead like you."

At that, Big Howie ran at me, and knocked me over. He fell on me and punched me in the face. Instinctively, my hands went up to protect my face, but that was about all I could do to defend myself, while Randy and two other guys pulled Big Howie off me. Big Howie pointed a fat finger at me and said, "You wait till after the game." One of his teammates added, "That's right Howie, finish the game and then kick his Jew ass."

I wasn't sure if I should wait. John, our team captain, asked me if I wanted to take a break, and I said, "No."

Randy said, "That other jerk who opened his mouth is Sam Salinas. He's a troublemaker and an instigator, and he's always goding Big Howie on."

Chucky told me, "You hit him good on that tackle. Don't let him scare you."

So the game went on. When the ball was snapped, I tried to get past my blocker to get to Big Howie, but I couldn't. They got a first down. On the next play I hit the kid who was blocking me with everything I had. But he had the same idea, which resulted in him going forward and me going backward. I decided to try something different, and on second down, when the ball was snapped, I moved forward, then backward to the right, and then flew through an opening straight at Big Howie, but just a bit from the side. He didn't see me coming, and as he started to put his hand up to throw, I jumped and got hold of his neck, and down he went. And pretty easily at that. As we both fell, he fell on top of me. As he got up, he punched me in the stomach and in the side, and then when standing, he kicked me in the groin. Randy and some of my teammates ran over to me, as I got up slowly holding my groin and hurting. It hurt enough to cry, but I didn't. There's no crying in football.

Big Howie was standing with his teammates, the only one grinning. Sam Salinas stood beside him, gloating. I took my hand away from my groin and walked back for the huddle. John, our team captain, told me to take a five-minute breather. Randy told me to keep my eye on the next play. Chucky said, "That's right, Larry, you watch the next play. You'll like it."

On the next play, the line-up seemed the same. I noticed nothing different, except that they gave Big Howie so much time that he was able to throw the ball long and high to a receiver who was free and clear. But a second or two after Big Howie let the ball fly, while everyone on the other team had their eyes on the ball, four of my teammates, with Chucky Padulowski leading the pack, tackled Big Howie. As they did, the rest of my teammates piled on. Everyone on my team, except for me, piled on Big Howie. They ripped the sweatshirt right off his back. A number of guys got in some good punches to the face and head, a few gave him some nasty kicks, and the last guy off, Chucky Padulowski, kicked Big Howie hard in the groin. Then they walked back to where I stood in astonishment; they just sneered and grinned as Big Howie got up very slowly holding his groin, his face red and bruised, and his sweatshirt torn and lying on the grass. He looked at the group of them standing there next to me, and then like a mad bull, seeing red all over, he started running toward me. Not them, but me.

Football was not my game, but when it came to running I was very fast. As a matter of fact, out of this group of twenty-five, I was probably among the fastest. So I took off down the field with Big Howie in pursuit, knowing that he could never catch me. When I got near the end of the field, I slowed down, and when Big Howie got close to me, I started running back toward the guys, with Big Howie still in pursuit. I didn't run too fast, just fast enough so that Big Howie couldn't catch me. I passed the guys, and then so did Big Howie. As I was running, I tripped on a good-sized rock and fell down. As I got up, I picked up the rock, with Howie just about seven feet from me and coming at me, full steam ahead. I held the rock up and as Big Howie ran at me, I did a quick move to the right just before impact, and tripped him with my foot. As he staggered and fell, I hit him very hard with the rock on or behind his left ear. He went down holding his ear and screeching in pain. I stood over him and held on to the rock in case he tried to get up, but he didn't. At that point Randy ran over and told me to get out of there fast and go home. I dropped the rock on the ground and left.

11

I had entered East High School in September of 1958. It was located between 3rd and 4th Streets off 27th Avenue East, in the East End area of Duluth. A few blocks southeast on 28th Avenue was London Road overlooking Lake Superior. There were some beautiful homes on London Road, huge mansions overlooking the lake. I'd think about what it would feel like to be living in one of those lakeshore mansions. I would imagine being lulled to sleep by gentle waves splashing against the rocky lakeshore, and evening breezes gusting off the big lake. I could then see myself awakening to a glistening pool of beautiful blue water as far as the eye could see, and being energized by the reflection of warm yellow sunlight from the lake's shimmering surface. That wouldn't be hard to get used to. Maybe I could talk Ruby into buying a Duluth mansion on London Road. It was nice to daydream.

East High School was in a great location. Lake Superior and many majestic mansions were on one side, and the University of Minnesota, Duluth Campus was on the other. It was an easy walk to the university after school, and I'd enjoy watching the tennis team go through their drills and practice matches. I would have loved to play like that. Sometimes I wandered over to where the University chess team met and watched them play. I'd just keep quiet and watch and watch, and after a while someone would ask if I'd like to play. It became one of my regular routines, playing chess with the U of M chess team. At first I won more games than I lost. After a while, I hardly lost any games. They knew I was from East High School, and that I was a member of the chess team there. I gave out that information freely. At East High School, out of five starting players, I played the third board position in my freshman year. In match play, I won every game I played against the other third board players from the other high schools. In my sophomore year I was co-captain of the chess team and played second board. I did not lose any match games all year. In my junior year I became captain of the chess team and played first board. I won all match games, and our team came in first place in the city. There was plenty of fuss, and East High School received a huge trophy with an inscription that read "First Place Chess Championship—Duluth, MN 1961."

1961 was a wonderful year for me—the chess championship and Ellen. That's when I first met Ellen. Ellen Westphal was on East High School's girls' tennis team, and out of a roster of 13 players, she was a solid number 6. In match play against other high schools, she had always played doubles and now and then singles as well. She played a tough game, and she was also very pretty.

One day, Randy had caught me watching the girls' tennis team practice. "Thinking of joining the team, Larry? You'd never make it. Legs too hairy, chest too flat, and too ugly."

I nodded agreement as I gave him the finger, and pointed to Ellen. "Who's that?"

"That's Ellen Westphal, very smart, very good tennis player, and kind of funny-looking."

There was nothing funny-looking about Ellen to me. I thought she was beautiful.

I joined East High School's boys' tennis team in my junior year in 1961, and out of a roster of 12, I was number 13. The coach said that I played tennis like I was playing handball, and my form and swing were an abomination and atrocious. He was also our English teacher, and he had a pretty good sense of humor. So, I asked him which one was an abomination and which one was atrocious. He grinned, gave me a coach's tap on the shoulder and said, "Either or both." He was right about handball. Back in Brooklyn, I had played regularly at the handball courts by the boardwalk near Coney Island. I had probably played for an hour or two each day, and easily for five or six hours every weekend.

The tennis coach also said that I was a tough competitor, gave 100 percent all the time, and never gave up. I even won a few sets here and there. He said that I should take lessons and practice if I wanted to play real tennis. I hadn't thought about taking tennis lessons. But I thought about Ellen playing tennis. She was a very good player, and I knew that I wanted to become a good tennis player also. Still, I wasn't keen on taking lessons, but I liked the idea of practicing. I obtained a Tennis Self-Taught book, and with the use of a ball machine I practiced hitting and serving close to ten hours a week. I really hit it hard during the year of 1961, and the coach started me in many doubles matches. He even let me get murdered in a couple of singles matches as well. He said I played a good game of tennis, and even though my form and swings were strange, I was a tough opponent.

I actually met Ellen Westphal later that school year. During a mixed tennis match, she said hello to me and introduced herself. She congratulated me on our first place chess championship. I thanked her and said she was a great tennis player and I enjoyed watching her. I corrected myself and said, "I meant watching you play." She asked me if I had picked up any pointers, and I said that my game was hopeless. She giggled and said, "Not hopeless, but definitely different. I'm on court now. See you later."

I saw Ellen now and then during my junior year at East. I strategically planned to bump into her by accident, so I could see her and say hello. There had been a lot of "hellos" and "see yous," but not much in between. I really wanted to talk to her, but I didn't know what to say. I had thought about asking her out, but I couldn't get up enough nerve to do so. I told Randy about my interest in Ellen, and he said, "She's very nice, real smart, and kind of a quiet girl. Why don't you call her up for a date?"

"No, I can't do that. I'm not ready. It's not the right time." I had all the excuses.

Randy kept bugging me and told me that he'd ask her out for me if I wanted. I thought he was kidding, but I wasn't sure. He was beginning to get on my nerves. I told him testily, "Enough already, just let it be. I'm not ready yet. So just forget it! Okay? I'll ask her out as soon as I'm ready."

12

In that same year, a fire had raged through and destroyed the chemistry lab and some adjoining classrooms at East High School. Early one Saturday morning I heard fire engine sirens screaming loudly. They seemed close enough for the fire to be in our own house or in the house next door. I ran outside and heard someone say that the high school was on fire. I told Dad that I'd be back, grabbed my bike, and took off toward East High School. There were three fire trucks there and a small group of spectators, maybe five or six people watching intently. Howie Simkey was there among them. The firemen had moved quickly, fire engines were positioned, ladders were extended upward, and in practically no time, a steady stream of water, a very forceful spray, had been directed toward a window on the third floor of the high school's west wing. I was thinking about the layout of the school in that area, and hoping that it was the English room where they taught poetry that was on fire, but no such luck. It was the chemistry room. By this time, there was a sizable crowd watching as a heavy spray of water doused the flames, and black and yellowish smoke with a stinky rotten egg–like smell billowed from the window above. It wasn't a pretty sight.

I had strategically positioned myself close to the adolescent contingent. There must have been about fifteen kids watching now, mostly kids from the high school, with a smattering of grade school kids as well. There were still some flames to be seen, but mostly smoke. The amount of smoke pouring out from the opening in the building that used to be a window was unbelievable. I heard Big Howie talking excitedly about the fire to a few of the high school kids, two of whom I recognized and knew. He was saying something about an explosion and then fire and flames all over the place. I didn't remember hearing an explosion. He then said, "Well, we can kiss our chemistry projects good-bye. And so much for our test scores. Up in flames and gone," he said to the three astonished faces.

When I returned home, I had breakfast with my family, and told them about the fire, and all that black and yellowish smelly smoke. Dad said that this was the first time there had ever been a fire at East High School. He thought it was strange that it had happened on a Saturday morning, what with nobody at the school. "Sounds suspicious to me," Ruby had said.

That morning after breakfast, the more I thought about the fire, the more suspicious it seemed. I mean I had gotten there pretty fast, but Howie was already there. And Howie lived further from the school than I did. How had he gotten there so fast? Also, what had he meant about an explosion and flames? How did he know about an explosion?

I remembered hearing or reading something about a person committing a crime and returning to the scene of the crime. Then I remembered Friday's little incident at the high school during chemistry class. Our teacher, Mr. Williams, had identified a number of outstanding and/or incomplete assignments that needed to be finished and turned in by Monday. Three students had been cited. Big Howie was one of them. I remembered Howie saying under his breath, "Yeah, we'll see about that shit," just loudly enough for some of his classmates, me included, to hear.

And just loudly enough to have caused Mr. Williams to look in Howie's direction and ask, "Howard, did you have something to add?"

But there had been no response from Howard. What had Howie meant by his comment, "We'll see about that shit?"

Based upon my observations and what I had heard Howie say, I believed that it was he who had started the fire. I couldn't confront him, but I couldn't let him get away with it either. I painstakingly listed all the facts that I knew and arranged what evidence I had by date and time. I was very careful to annotate exactly what I'd heard and exactly what I'd seen. I reviewed what I'd written a number of times to make sure it was accurate and complete, and that nothing was left out. I had included the names of the high schoolers to whom Howie had directed his remarks about the explosion and the flames. I also included the names of the classmates who were close enough to Howie to hear him say, "We'll see about that shit." I called the high school principal at his home and shared my thoughts and suspicions with him. He listened, thanked me for calling, and suggested that we meet at the Duluth police station. He asked if he could speak to my father.

I gave Ruby a ten-second summation of the situation and handed him the phone. He listened, frowned, frowned some more and said, "Okay, we'll see you in about an hour." He said to me, "Okay, Larry, tell me what you know."

"Well, Dad, it's like this. When you said, 'A fire on Saturday morning, nobody at the school, sounds suspicious to me,' I got to thinking. And everything I thought of led to Howie Simkey. So I wrote it all down. Here, see."

Dad squinted at my scribbles and frowned. I thought I detected a sliver of a smile, but I couldn't be sure. After he finished reading he queried only half jokingly, "Okay, Perry Mason, we've got a little visit to the police station to make. Are you going to be okay?"

I nodded and quipped back, "I'll be okay, Dad, but '77 Sunset Strip' is more my style than 'Perry Mason.'"

Larry Stoller

At the station I told the police everything I knew. I answered their questions and gave them my notes of what I had heard and observed on specific dates and at corresponding times. They asked me where I'd been before the sirens started. Before I could answer, Ruby spoke up, saying I'd been at home. I nodded in agreement.

Word had it that Howie was called in and interviewed by the police that same day. Accompanied by his father, he denied any knowledge of the fire. He said that he'd been riding his bike, heard the fire engine sirens, and got to the fire right after the trucks did. When asked about the explosion, he said he thought he'd heard one. When asked where he'd been before the fire engine sirens, he said he'd been just riding around. When asked what he'd meant by his remark at school on Friday, "Yeah, we'll see about that shit," he said he didn't remember saying that. The police had also interviewed the other high school kids who witnessed the fire. They had confirmed Howie's remarks about kissing the chemistry projects and test scores good-bye.

On the following Monday, the news from the school grapevine was that the principal had Howie in the office and was getting ready to kick him out of school. The grapevine was not totally accurate. The school principal did have Howie in the office and asked him what he'd meant by the remark, "Yeah, we'll see about that shit." Again

Howie denied having said that, and he demanded to know who it was that had stooled on him. He also told the principal that no one could prove anything and that they had nothing on him. The word around the school was that the principal was furious and that he warned Howie that he would be watching him closely. If there were any problems, out he'd go. Most everyone in the school believed that Howie had set the fire, but no one had seen him do it, and without any concrete evidence, he was never charged.

13

In the beginning of my senior year at East High, I was at a tennis team practice while the girls' tennis team was practicing across the way. I wasn't able to concentrate on hitting the ball because I kept looking at Ellen. When the girls' team took a break, I saw Ellen get a drink of water and sit down to rest. I stopped practicing and ran over to her and smiled and said hello. She looked tired but really happy to see me, and she smiled back and said, "Hi, how are you, Larry?"

Without thinking, I replied, "I'm okay, but I could be better."

She looked at me, a little puzzled.

With my foot stuck in my mouth I explained, "I mean I could be better if, Well, I was wondering if, Would it be okay if." I just couldn't get the damn words out of my mouth. It was like time was moving faster than I could speak. I was moving my lips, but I couldn't say the words fast enough to finish what I wanted to say. Speech and time were out of synch. I finally managed to ask, "Would it be okay if I called you at home?"

I don't know how it sounded or if it came out clearly enough to be understood, but Ellen smiled and said, "I'd like that. I'd really like that. Got to get back to practice. Talk to you soon."

Just as Ellen was about to go, one of the girls from her tennis team trotted over to us. She was tall and wiry—taller than I was. Her arms looked strong, almost muscular. Her hair was jet black and her skin dark olive. She looked more like a high school teacher than a high school student.

She stared at me and spoke to Ellen, "Is this guy bothering you?"

Ellen replied, "No, Rose. This is Larry. Larry, this is Rose."

Before I could say hello, Rose looked away and said, "Come on Ellen, we have to get back to practice." And then she left.

Ellen looked embarrassed as she said, "I'd better get back, Larry. I'm sorry about Rose. I don't know what got into her. Call me tonight."

I thought about Rose. What a witch. What a bitch. Then I thought about Ellen and forgot about Rose.

That evening at home, I had to rethink what I had said and what she had said. I should have said, "Would it be okay if I called you at home to ask you if you'd like to go out sometime?" That's what I should have said. Darn it, I forgot to say the "go out" part. What if I called her, which she said was okay to do, and asked her if she would like to go out and she said no. I blew it. I should have asked her then and there if she'd like to go out. Well, maybe not. That would be rushing her. After an hour of thinking I should have said this or I should have said that, I realized that I was alone in the house. I checked the other rooms to make sure. There was no one around, but I had noticed something odd. Although we had only one telephone in the house, it seemed to appear in all of the rooms. I wondered why my mind was playing tricks on me. I sat down and held the telephone in between my hands and stared at it. And then I called Ellen.

This was the first time I had called a girl at home for a date, and it wasn't easy to do. Her mom answered, and I wanted to hang up, but I said hello and asked if Ellen was in. Her mom asked, "Who's this?"

I said, "Larry Stone from school."

I heard her call out, "Ellen, it's Larry Stone from school," loud enough I thought for anyone and everyone to hear. I felt a little embarrassed. Ellen picked up the phone and said hello. It sounded strange to hear her voice on the phone, but it sounded wonderful also. This was also the first time I was really alone with Ellen. There was no one else around. I said, "This is Larry from school."

She said, "I know."

Crap, why did I repeat "This is Larry from school"? That was stupid. I started to feel embarrassed again, but I forced myself to relax and say, "I'm calling because I wanted to talk to you and ask you if you'd like to go out with me." The words almost didn't make it out of my mouth.

She said, "I'd love to. When?"

I confirmed in my brain that she had said, "I'd love to," and I said, "Saturday. This Saturday. But if you can't this Saturday, then next Saturday."

"This Saturday is good, Larry."

Feeling more confident, I said, "How about a movie and then something to eat or something to eat and then a movie?"

"Sounds great, Larry!"

"Okay, Ellen. I'll come by at 6 p.m." Jeez, what'd I say "p.m." for? I'm not going to come by at 6 a.m.

"Okay, Larry, see you then."

I remained seated, feeling pretty good about myself and how things had gone on the telephone. However, as the realization that Ellen and I would be going out together on Saturday began to sink in, the anticipation of our first date became overwhelming. I wished that it was Saturday already. To make matters worse, I became anxious, thinking about what I should wear. What worried me was that since I didn't know what she would be wearing, how would I know what to wear.

So now I'm thinking, it will be Saturday in no time, and I don't know what to wear. I wasn't looking forward to asking Randy for advice, but I was desperate. When he returned home, I waited until he was alone, and then I approached him with my dilemma.

He asked me where we were going on the

date, and I told him that we were going to a movie and then to the malt shop. He asked me if I had a dark brown corduroy sport jacket with elbow patches, matching light brown corduroy slacks, a white turtleneck sweater, and brown and white checkered socks. I told him that I didn't think so. He then asked me if I had some sexy red bikini briefs and burst out laughing. I now realized that he had been jerking me around from the beginning. Even though he was only kidding, and come to think of it, it was pretty funny, all I could see was his neck and my hands around his neck strangling him. I think he saw what I saw also, and in between laughing, trying to stop laughing, and apologizing, he told me to just wear casual slacks, a sport shirt, a sweater, and comfortable loafers and that would be fine!

That Saturday night we saw the movie *Paris Blues*. It was kind of a double romance, and it had a great jazz score. We held hands during the movie. After the movie, we had sandwiches and malts at the local soda fountain. Some of our friends saw us and waved and said hello. I don't think anyone noticed or even cared about what I was wearing. Big Howie saw me and sneered at me. I was thinking, there must be a big rock around here somewhere. After we ate, we walked and talked. We talked a lot. Ellen shared her plans for college with me. She would go to the University of Minnesota in Duluth and become a psychologist. I asked her how she knew that she wanted to become a psychologist. She said that she enjoyed working with people and that she would like to help people lead happier and healthier lives. She asked about my plans. I had to admit that I was not sure what I wanted to do. However, I indicated that I also planned to attend the University of Minnesota, and that maybe after a year or so I would know what I wanted to do. I think I talked too much. It was easy to talk to Ellen and to listen to her as well.

I got Ellen back to her house a little past 11:15 that evening. As we approached her doorstep, I looked at her pretty face and said, "I had a great time."

She said, "So did I."

I let go of her hand and said goodnight. I moved closer to her to kiss her, but I couldn't do it. I moved my head a little closer to hers, but I still couldn't conjure up enough nerve to kiss her. I had not anticipated that there would be a kiss, and therefore a kissing problem on our first date. I was looking at her and thinking about where to kiss her. On the cheek or the forehead? That would be pretty safe. Not on the nose. That would be stupid. On the lips? That's what I'd like to do but do I dare? I was feeling very stupid, standing there and staring at her, but not doing anything. Suddenly, in one smooth, graceful, forceful, but gentle motion, Ellen put her arms around me, kissed me full on the lips, said goodnight, and disappeared into the house. It all happened so quickly that I didn't have a chance to kiss her back. It was wonderful! I'd never felt like that before. It took all of five seconds, but it was the best five seconds of my life. Damn, why didn't I kiss her back! It took about twenty seconds to break the trance, and then I realized I was still standing on her doorstep and staring at her door. I left to go home. I was the happiest man in the world.

Ellen and I were inseparable during our senior year in high school. I gave her a gold ankle bracelet. It took me a while to find the right one. But I found exactly what I was looking for, and Ellen loved it and always wore it. We were going steady. Between going out, playing tennis, and getting ready for college, we were almost always together. I didn't play much chess in my senior year, but it didn't matter to me. Being with Ellen was what mattered. And being with Ellen was great.

14

The angry voice that spoke was filled with jealousy and hate.

"That goddamn Larry Stone. I don't know what Ellen sees in him. He's not even from Duluth. He's from New York. And he's a Jew. How could she stand being seen with him? She should be with me. I could make her happy.

"But what chance do I have now? The two of them are always together. He takes her out almost every weekend, and to make matters worse, he gave her an ankle bracelet. Now they are going steady. Damn him!

"What right does he have to even be here in Duluth? He should have stayed in New York with the rest of the Jews. I don't know why the Johnsons ever took him in in the first place. They never should have.

"Ellen is different from most of the other girls. She's more mature, intelligent, and refined. Before Stone, she wasn't seeing anyone. I'm sure she would have been ready for my kind of love and companionship in her senior year. I know I could have made her happy. She was ready for a relationship and I was ready to approach her. Then this no good Jew starts seeing her and all of a sudden, the two of them are in love. I wish I

could snap my fingers and make him disappear. Or send him back to New York where he belongs. Maybe he'll just drop dead or get hit by a car or something. I wish he was dead!"

15

I had been fourteen when I resettled in Duluth and too young to really sell real estate. My dad, Ruby Johnson, had a medium-sized real estate company called All Duluth Realty, and he would talk about business now and then. In my freshman year at East High School, one evening during dinner, Ruby was telling us about a new listing he had picked up in the West End area of Duluth. He liked to share his business stories with the family, and we liked to listen to them. His new listing was a dilapidated three-bedroom, one-bath, one-and-a-half-story home. It was solid enough and in an area of nicely kept one-and-a-half-story homes. Although these were older homes, they were in a good location and an attractive-looking neighborhood, one in which neighborhood pride showed. But this house needed a new roof, exterior and interior painting, some minor mechanical repairs, and a lot of cosmetic fixes. Ruby suggested that cosmetically, the house needed a good makeover or possibly a total facelift. He had had the listing for a month now. There had been some showings but no second showings. Realtor feedback included statements like "We got there, and the buyer decided not to look inside," and there were a lot of negative comments. There was not an offer in sight and no prospect of one either. Ruby explained that the sellers had no money to fix up the house. Then he shook his head back and forth and said, "What to do? What to do?"

As I listened, I wanted to help, but what did I know about selling houses? Not much. But I had an idea. So I spoke up, "Why not rent out the house to someone who would promise to buy it in the future?" I explained my idea. "A short-term rental. Rent it to someone who wants to own but can't afford to right now, to someone who has a steady job and wants a home for himself and his family. Someone who is very handy. Rent it for less than it would normally rent for and make up a list of things that the renter would have to do to fix it up, little by little, by such and such a date. But the renter would have to agree that by a certain date he would buy the house. Maybe use some of the rent for the renter to buy the house. Maybe even increase the price of the house, since this is a special deal for the renter. By the time the renter buys the house, the house will be worth more, because of the repairs and updates made by the renter. It would be a chance for a family to own their own home in the near future instead of forever renting. They could live in it now and own it later."

Ruby smiled and said, "A rent with an option to buy. Even get a better price for the house, but work the buyer into the house now." He took out an ad and netted a slew of prospective future buyers who wanted to become homeowners. He picked the most promising and best-qualified buyer, and six months later, closed the deal, getting more for the seller than the original list price. On the day of the closing, Ruby gave me $250, my share of the commission for helping to sell the house. That was easy money. I liked selling real estate.

16

Ruby let Randy and me help out around the office. We were like apprentices. We would learn a lot about the real estate business, and we would get paid a little now and then as well. Very erratic income, this real estate income, so Randy worked at a local supermarket packing groceries and delivering them to people's homes. It was steady income, good money, with tips also. I got a job at the local movie house and continued to help out at the real estate office as well. It was crummy money at the movie house and no tips, but I never missed any movies. I saw all the new features, over and over again.

In my senior year at East High School, Ruby was telling Randy and me about a new listing that he would be picking up. "Everything's signed, and it will go on the market in about two weeks. That's when the owners want to start showing it. A nice expensive home in the Hillside area of Duluth, a place where lawyers and doctors live. It should go for about $150,000. Wouldn't that be a honey to hog!" And then Ruby started making hog-like sounds, oink-oink, aghh-aghh, oink-oink. "Just imagine listing that baby and bringing in the buyer as well. That'd be about a $9,000 commission! Aghh-aghh-aghh, oink-oink-oink."

BROKER'S OPEN

I had another idea. I shared it with Ruby, "Why not get a picture and description of the house, an attractive collage of the outside and inside of the house. Have it professionally done and put together a super sales letter. Send it to all the doctors and lawyers in Duluth, asking them if they would like to live in that house in the Hillside area of Duluth." I asked Ruby if I could try that angle. He agreed but said that both Randy and I should work on it, and that he needed to see and approve everything we did before anything went out.

I got the names, addresses, and phone numbers of all the doctors and lawyers in Duluth from the Duluth Yellow Pages. I typed up mailing labels and made copies of the phone book pages that I could use for record-keeping purposes. Ruby had some beautiful pictures of the house, just the outside, but from many appealing angles. This house had great curb appeal. The front yard was handsomely landscaped, and the back yard overlooked the woods. Ruby also had all the house details and statistics from the listing sheet (number of bedrooms, number of baths, additional rooms, room dimensions, total finished square feet, number of fireplaces, size of garage, lot size, updates, and special features). Randy had a knack for graphics, and he organized the pictures in a beautiful collage layout. He knew someone at the high school who did calligraphy, and we hired her to pen the house facts and features in, next to and around the pictures. It looked like a piece of artwork that could be framed. Using a top-of-the-line IBM typewriter, I composed a descriptive and personal sales letter. I included information about the house, its history, its amenities, and an invitation to contact Ruby for a private and selective showing.

Ruby had seven selective showings during the next two weeks and sold the house in the second week for a full price offer. He picked up a 6 percent commission on $150,000, a cool $9,000. When the deal closed, he oinked and aghhed all the way to the bank.

Ruby was so pleased that he went out and purchased a new Chrysler Newport 300. It was a beautiful car, a classic white sedan, with power windows and push-button transmission. He paid $2,964.00 for the car at Dokmo Motors, a great price.

Randy and I received $1,250 each! There's definitely something to this business of selling houses.

17

I attended the University of Minnesota, Duluth Campus, from 1962 to 1966. Like Ellen, I majored in psychology and received a Bachelor of Science degree in June 1966. Psychology interested me for a number of reasons. I was always curious about why people behaved in the way that they did, and I felt that understanding people better would be of value to me in business and in selling real estate. I also thought that a degree in psychology would be a good springboard for me if I decided to pursue other types of work. And then there was Ellen. Maybe we'd be in a couple of classes together.

During those four years, I completed several minor courses in sociology and criminology. The criminal mentality fascinated me. I wanted to know what made the criminal mind tick. The smarts could be the same, the IQs equivalent, so why the deviant behavior, why choose the criminal path? What exactly did the criminal psyche look like?

During college, I sold a lot of real estate, and made some serious money. I worked residential real estate only, listing and selling existing homes. I scheduled my real estate appointments around my college classes. My classes were in the mornings and in the early afternoons and my appointments were in the late afternoons and in the evenings. Occasionally, there would be a conflict, and I would have to decide between going to the class or going on the appointment. It got to be quite a juggling act, especially keeping those "studying" and "writing paper" balls in the air without dropping them. About 75 percent of my clients were sellers, and the remaining 25 percent buyers. Oftentimes, sellers became buyers. Every now and then I'd come across someone who wanted to build a new home. Since Randy was more interested in new home construction and new home development, I would refer my new home prospects to him. Architecture and drafting were Randy's forte.

I became an expert hogger and was obsessed with selling the homes that I listed. Bringing in my own buyers became my top priority. In fact, I was very successful in finding my own buyers for some of the homes I listed. Ruby kept telling me to go after the listings and get as many as I could, that is where the big dollars are. "Let someone else sell your listing. They get the buyer, you get the money. Don't worry so much about selling all your own listings. Get a good volume of steady listings and you'll be making some serious money," he would say. I knew he was right, but for me to list a home and then sell it myself was an incredibly satisfying experience.

So I continued to list homes, but spent a lot of

time cultivating buyers in the hope that I could sell them one of my listings. Sometimes I think I frustrated Ruby a little with my business philosophy, but I was doing well and making good money. My hogger rate, as I referred to it, was about 15 percent (which even impressed Ruby). And I was happy doing what I was doing. Besides, when I made money, Ruby made money. So we were both happy with the way business was going.

The key to being an expert hogger could be found in a routine four-part formula. Although it could be boring at times, it worked and made money for me. So I followed it religiously:

Part 1–Cultivate and accumulate good buyers and sell them something as soon as possible.
Part 2–Match your buyers to your own listings. If there is a fit, sell them your own listing. If not, sell them some other listing or find them a home.
Part 3–For listings with no buyers, target market to potential buyers using word-of-mouth, direct mail, or newspaper advertising.
Part 4–Do parts 1, 2, and 3 every single day!

Part 1 was farming plain and simple. Renters were my seeds, and I grew them into different kinds of buyers. I concentrated heavily on my renters, using direct mail pieces to contact them. I developed my own mailing list using the Polk directories, and sent periodic mailings to Duluth apartment houses. I would always call the apartment manager first and ask how much the rentals were for one, two, or three-bedroom apartments. This was valuable in determining good fits between buyers and houses. Based upon the amount of rent paid, I was able to develop a price range by specific apartment house of how much specific renters could afford in terms of house payments.

My direct mail message was always the same, owning was better than renting. First, keep your hard-earned money instead of giving it away as rent. I'd explain that money put into owning a house would eventually be returned when it was sold. Second, the home would appreciate and build up equity for the owner. I'd further explain that owning a house was like having a big savings account. The analogy I would use went something like this: "Imagine that your house is worth $50,000 and it's appreciating 5 percent per year, that's $2,500 you're making in equity in the first year. And in each succeeding year, your equity will increase because your house will be worth more." I would explain that there were tax savings in owning, and I would show how much money a homeowner could get back each year. I would always offer to provide a free, no-hassle, no-obligation pre-qualification for them, and show them how much money a mortgage company would be willing to lend them based upon their income and debt. I had specially prepared sheets that started out stating, "YOU CAN AFFORD THIS MUCH HOUSE." I'd sit down with them, take about fifteen minutes of their time to fill in the sheet, and then I'd affix a label right on the sheet with a loan officer's name and telephone number whom they could call to get a loan to buy a house. Once they got verbal approval, and I got the verbal okay from the bank, we would then get together, see what was available, and go look at houses. I had three different loan officers I was working with, and I would attach the label of the loan officer who I felt would best satisfy the mortgage needs of the specific prospective buyer. I would then contact the loan officer and give them the buyer's name, address, and telephone number. The idea was to get the prospective buyer and loan officer together as soon as possible. Once the buyers had verbal approval, we'd go out house shopping.

Part 2 involved matching and marketing. If I had any approved buyers or soon-to-be-approved buyers who might be interested in any of my listings, I would call them and tell them about the homes. I found that as long as I was low-key, most prospective buyers were very interested in knowing what was available. If there was any interest, we would go to look at the homes. If they were not interested in any of my listings, they would be quick to tell me why. That's one way I would find out exactly what kind of home they were looking for and what they really wanted in a home. I'd add their particular needs to their profile (their requirements and preferences, which I kept on a separate large index card) and follow up by sending them a list of homes that better met their needs. They'd review the list, maybe do a drive-by, and I'd call them to find out which ones they wanted to see. Then we'd set up the showings and go look at the homes. As soon as they saw the home they liked, and mentally purchased it, then I'd physically sell it to them. That was pretty much the routine.

Part 3 included target marketing via direct mail. Of the listings I had, for which I did not have any ready buyers, I would determine—guesstimate might be a better word—what kind of person would want to buy this home. I would then use direct mail to reach that specific market segment and advertise the home accordingly. I'd also use newspaper advertising to try to find my own buyers for a home before some other agent found a buyer.

Part 4 was the hardest of all to do. That was to keep doing parts 1, 2, and 3. No matter how I looked at it, it always boiled down to the three P's, PERSISTENCE, PERSISTENCE, and PERSISTENCE.

18

Ellen and I saw each other all during college. We were still going steady and we loved being together. But both of us were so busy with college courses, exams, and outside jobs, that our going steady seemed more like sporadic dating. Still, we only saw each other, and when we did, the air around us was filled with electricity and our bodies were like magnets that clung tightly together.

Yet something was changing between us. It began a couple of months into our junior year. On occasion, and then increasing in frequency, Ellen would comment that she felt that I was obsessed with real estate, and that real estate always came first in my life, even before her. I would get defensive, and point out to her that she was involved in so many extra-curricular psychology activities and volunteer groups that we hardly had any time to be together. And it went on and on like that. I think it was a time in our lives when we were growing in different directions, developing new interests, and taking on more responsibilities. And in a way, we got jealous of this growth and the interests and responsibilities that went along with it. We never realized how indifferent time was to accommodating our needs, and how unforgiving as well.

At the end of our senior year, we still loved each other, without fully understanding love, but our lives and circumstances were changing. Graduation and the summer would soon be upon us. In a few weeks, Ellen would be off to Europe for a month, a graduation gift from her parents. And I was going to see the world as well, through a four-year hitch in the United States Navy. It was my choice to join the Navy. I felt that it was better to choose your military service than to get drafted and have no choice.

My hitch started a week before Ellen's trip. We spent the night before I left together in a lovely room in an elegant hotel and said good-bye to each other all through the night. We talked and then made love. We cried and then made love again. We loved each other, as the night became morning. We held each other as the sun began its upward climb. It was a spectacular sunrise, bringing brightness and happiness to a clear blue sky, unlike our faces, which were drawn and sad. We dressed, hugged, kissed, and said good-bye again. There are so many ways to say good-bye.

Ellen drove off with tears in her eyes. I waved and wiped the tears from mine.

19

In the United States Navy, I was assigned to Naval Intelligence. The assignment included collecting and reviewing information and conducting periodic investigations and audits to ensure the safety and safekeeping of naval personnel and equipment. It was interesting work and it required that I visit numerous naval shipyards and warehouses. Many of them were stateside, but now and then I received overseas assignments. During these assignments, I interacted with a variety of naval personnel— officers and enlisted men and women. Although I was never attached to a specific ship for an extended period of time, I was on many different types of ships. I was familiar with the physical layout of all ships in the fleet. I was also familiar with the number and type of personnel that were on these ships, with the respective equipment, with the administrative chain of command, and with the respective policies and procedures. Although all of this information was included in countless pages of numerous manuals, most of it I committed to memory. When exceptions and/or operating anomalies were identified, my superiors would come to me before looking in the manuals. There were times when I thought my memory cells were in overload, and couldn't hold any more information. I would worry about waking up one day and not being able to retain or recall anything at all. But the brain is truly an amazing organ. There's almost no limit to what it can do when it's working well and working at full capacity.

For example, when I was playing chess in high school, my head was filled with chess strategies. I memorized all the chess openings for the beginning game, and I was still able to recall the best strategies to use during the middle game and end game. I was also able to respond to my opponent's moves by analyzing the alternatives and determining the best counter-moves.

When I started dating Ellen, in my senior year in high school, most of the chess information that I had stored in those memory cells was erased. During that last year in high school, my mind went on an extended vacation. It was filled with the happiness and the excitement of first love. I thought about Ellen most of the time, and every day was a good day for a daydream.

During college, my intellect was revived as I became busy with courses, tests, quizzes, papers, research projects, and the business of selling real estate. I still saw Ellen and thought about her, but daydreaming didn't result in getting good grades and earning good money.

In the Navy everything got turned upside down. It was like I was on a little island surrounded by water, ships, land, more water, and more ships. It seemed that the Navy was everywhere. My body and brain now belonged to Uncle Sam and my head became an exclusive repository for policies, procedures, facts, figures, and service-related statistics.

After four years in the Navy, I felt like a little fish in a big ocean, and I was ready to trade in my sea legs for some landlubber legs. I got back to Duluth and started selling real estate again. Getting back into real estate was easy. I sent out a carton of cards stating that I was back at All Duluth Realty, after serving four years in the Navy, to assist past and future clients with their real estate needs. Ruby was so happy that I was back at the brokerage that he took out a large advertisement in the *Duluth News Tribune*. It read, "All Duluth Realty Welcomes Back Larry Stone, Broker-Realtor, employed by Uncle Sam, United States Navy, for the past four years."

I also enrolled in the University of Minnesota's graduate school, in the master's degree program in psychology. I had found that my background in psychology, in addition to being useful in the real estate business, was also extremely helpful when I was conducting naval investigations. In fact, during my four-year stint, I had the opportunity to complete several courses in criminology and psychology at various naval training facilities.

I had lost touch with Ellen while I was in the service. In the beginning we'd written to each other quite often, but in the last two years we had not corresponded at all. I was pretty sure that we were not going steady anymore. That was evident from our being apart, but more so from our non-communication. I knew that while I was working for Uncle Sam, Ellen had completed her master's degree and was working at a well-known Duluth mental health clinic. I also knew that she had started on a doctoral degree program. It was Randy who would send me news about Ellen from time to time. Although I never asked for it, I never discouraged it. What I didn't know was that she was completing a twelve-month internship in Washington, D.C.

When I returned to Duluth and learned of her internship, I threw myself into selling real estate and attending graduate school. That was pretty much my life. The months passed quickly. Soon a year went by, and work and school consumed me.

I was still very competitive, and I worked day and night to find buyers for my listings. If someone else had a hot listing, I'd sometimes make believe it was mine, and I would transfer my workaholic energy to finding a buyer for that listing as well. When I was selling real estate, I was competing, and when I was competing, I was fierce.

During this time, I remember one multiple offer situation in which I presented my offer along with the listing agent's offer. The listing agent's name was William Preston. He was the broker-owner of William Preston—Prestigious Properties.

BROKER'S OPEN

He told me that there would be another offer presented in addition to mine, but he didn't tell me that the other offer was his. I arrived at the seller's home early and the sellers graciously invited me in. We got to talking, and I said that they were lucky to have two offers coming in. They said that William had indicated that he had a superb offer from one of his own clients, but that since there was another offer, we should look at both of them. I told them that I had a very good offer also, that my clients had a little four-year-old girl, and that the three of them had fallen in love with their home. I also mentioned that everything about their home was just right for my buyers, and that the fenced back yard was perfect for their little girl to play in. I showed them a picture of the family. It was a nice family picture, and the little girl was a real cutie. The sellers looked at the picture and told me that it reminded them of when their children were little. They added that their children used to play in the back yard all the time.

As they were reminiscing, William Preston showed up. He was surprised to see me there already, and he asked me what I was doing there. I told him that I had arrived earlier than I expected, and that the sellers had graciously invited me in. He nodded but he didn't look happy. He asked me for the purchase agreement and he suggested that I wait in the basement while he presented both offers. I told him absolutely not. I said that since we each had an offer, we should present our offers with everyone present—one first, then the other, and let the sellers ask any questions and decide what they wanted to do. The sellers chimed in and said that that was fine with them. Reluctantly, Preston agreed, but what choice did he have. It was up to the sellers on how to proceed.

Both offers were excellent—pre-approved buyers, good earnest money, good closing dates, and no contingencies. His clients were a couple with no children, and mine were a family of three. My offer was five hundred dollars more than his. The sellers decided to go with my offer. Preston said that his people would increase their offer by $1,000. I was about to say something. I knew that my people would meet that price, but I decided to keep quiet. I stared at Preston briefly and then looked at the sellers and smiled. It was the kind of smile that I hoped suggested that I would not respond, and that it was in their hands and up to them to decide. The sellers made a quick decision. They indicated that they would deal with what was brought to the table, and that they would go with my offer. That was that. My people got the house.

For me, there was always great satisfaction in getting a hogger. However, even though this was not a hogger, having my offer accepted over the the listing broker's offer was just as gratifying. As a matter of fact, in this particular instance, taking

William Preston's hogger away from him felt even better.

Ruby was happy with my real estate sales and successes, but he was also worried about me. He told me to relax a little and have some fun before I got burned out. So I started playing tennis again, and even a little chess now and then. But Ruby was right about "getting burned out." I was tired of real estate and I was tired of graduate school. I was also tired of Duluth.

Change was knocking at my door. It asked to come in, but I kept the door closed, and tried to ignore it. But the knocking kept getting louder and louder, so I finally opened the door. And when I did, change rushed in, and it was everywhere. It was inside my head and inside my body. It was telling me I needed to get up and go. It was saying that it was time to go somewhere else and do something different. And change would not leave me, until I left Duluth.

I had been here in Duluth, while Ellen was there in Washington. When I learned that Ellen had decided to stay in Washington for another six months or longer, I decided to test the water a little. I applied for some jobs there. I obtained some very good leads and even a couple of job offers, and I was thinking of leaving Duluth and moving to Washington, D.C.

I decided to call Ellen. I don't know why I hadn't called her sooner, but I got her number from her parents and called. She was surprised to hear from me after all these years. As we talked, I got the feeling that there was something that she wanted to tell me and that she was trying to figure out how to tell me. She mentioned that she was almost finished with her internship, and that she had decided to stay on for another six months before returning to Duluth. That I already knew. Her parents had mentioned it to me. She said, "There's something else I need to tell you, but it's difficult to say."

I told her that we had always been able to talk to each other about anything and that she should just say it. And she did. Ellen said that she had met someone in Washington, and that he was one of the reasons she was extending her stay for six months. She also said that she was engaged to be married and that when she returned to Duluth, they would be married and live here.

I had some very strange feelings stirring around inside me: anger, hurt, loss, and some others that I could not explain. I was momentarily unable to speak. I finally managed to say, "I'm very happy for you, Ellen. I really am. I always wanted you to be happy."

She said that she had always known that.

After that telephone conversation with Ellen, there was one thing I knew for sure. I could not be in Duluth when she returned, and I could not live in Duluth while she was here either. I decided I would move to Washington, D.C. It was kind of strange, she moves away, I move back, she moves back, and I move away. I accepted a job as a police psychologist with the Washington, D.C., Metropolitan Police Department. It appeared that the combination of my undergraduate degree, my Navy experience, the courses and programs that I'd completed in the service, and the graduate courses that I'd completed at the University of Minnesota qualified me for the job. I was hired under the condition that I would complete a master's degree program in psychology in D.C. during my first two years on the job. I was fine with that.

It seemed so ironic. Ellen would come back to Duluth to get married, settle down, and start her new life, and I would leave Duluth and go to D.C. to find whatever I was looking for. It wasn't really ironic at all. It was the easy way out, and I took it.

20

After eleven years as a police psychologist and homicide detective in Washington, D.C., what did I have to show for it? A disability retirement on 75 percent salary at thirty-nine years of age, and a shot-up body that was operating on one lung instead of two. Not to mention, no job, no career, and no prospect for either. I suppose I could have coasted and enjoyed life on my disability salary, but I wasn't ready to retire just yet.

I was heavy into the three R's, Resting, Relaxing, and Recuperating. I was recuperating on two levels—physically and mentally. But I considered myself fortunate. I was alive and on the road to recovery. I was in good shape financially. My home in Vienna, Virginia, was free and clear. The money my parents had left me, and the money I had made from selling real estate, was invested in stocks, mutual funds, and real estate. Thanks to Ruby's assistance and advice, in twenty years my investments had grown to a sum of $750,000. I had also made a number of friends over the past eleven years in D.C., a few of them close friends, who visited me regularly to see how I was doing.

My closest friend and confidant was Danny

O'Neill. Danny O'Neill was also known as "Dannyboy" within a small circle of his close friends. I was a member of that circle of friends, and that's what I called him.

Danny and I had joined the Washington, D.C., police force at about the same time. That's when we first met. We went to the police academy together, and it was there that we became good friends. Danny had spent four years in the Marines before joining the police force. In the United States Marines, Danny learned to deal with people and situations very directly, and sometimes abruptly as well. I thought about my military experience. From what I remembered, acting tactfully was pretty low on the list of desired behavioral traits. Danny told me that he needed to tone down his behavior a bit. I felt that he needed to modify his behavior more than a bit. He said that he wanted to be less confrontational, and he asked me if I could help him. So I taught him how to be tactful. I told Danny that being tactful was a "strategy-type-of-thing." It required "thinking before talking" and "thinking before doing." I taught Danny a little about the art of negotiating. I also explained to him that there was a time to go to the mat, but that most of the time you didn't have to go that far. Danny understood what I was saying, and he was able to modify his behavior accordingly. That, in part, helped him to get through the academy. At the same time that I was the teacher, I was also the student. Danny showed me that sometimes you had to stand tough, so that you were not taken advantage of. It made a lot of sense to me.

After the academy, our friendship grew stronger. On the job we respected each other's talents, and we always worked together to achieve our career goals and objectives. Before long, we were both working in homicide as detectives. Both Danny and I made Sergeant, and then I got promoted to Lieutenant. Danny would kid me and say, "Real police work takes some brains and a lot of brawn." He would then go on, "If you have too many brains they'll make you a lieutenant, and give you the administrative stuff to do." I would just look at him and smile wryly—"that Stone smile," that's what he used to call it. That would bug him no end. Dannyboy and I worked well together, and we liked each other. We watched each other's back. It felt good to have someone close by whom I could always trust.

Off the job we'd go out together socially. We got along well together. Danny said he liked the way I thought about things, and the way I figured things out as well. He said that I was able to see things differently and come up with ideas that others might never even dream of. He also said that some of my ideas were hard to follow, but that I was always willing to explain them. He appreciated that.

I liked Danny's direct approach and his ability to act and react very quickly. Danny liked to keep things simple, and he did an excellent job when it came to sizing up people and situations. Danny was also popular with the ladies. He stood about 5'6"; he was trim and very muscular, and he had short red hair. He had been a gymnast in high school, and he had also been on the Olympic circuit for a couple of years. When we went out together, it was unbelievable the way women would gravitate toward him and check him out. It was like he was this powerful magnet, and the women were pieces of light metal that were drawn to him.

I remember one time when we went to Hilton Head Island, South Carolina, for a week vacation. These women were all over him. I would think to myself, women adored Dannyboy. They would look at him and they would see a very trim and muscular Adonis, whom they wanted to wrap up and take home with them. One thing I knew for sure. Whenever Danny and I would go somewhere, there was never a shortage of women. That was okay with me.

Things really changed for Danny in 1981. Over the years, he had earned a reputation as an extremely effective and efficient "doer." If one needed a specific job done and done right, Danny O'Neill was the man. Danny had been given a long-term special assignment—to provide protection for high-ranking diplomats visiting the nation's capital. With a small group of handpicked police personnel, Danny had been extremely successful. During one particular assignment, Danny's contingent had been escorting a high-ranking Sudan oil minister from Washington National Airport to his country's embassy, and then from the embassy to the hotel where he and his family would be staying. On the grounds in front of the embassy, a man in a black garment and white turban came from nowhere, and rushed toward the minister with a knife in his hand. Immediately Danny got in front of the minister, disarmed and incapacitated the attacker in a lightning-quick movement, and had his men remove the assailant, while ushering the minister and his family into the embassy. The minister was extremely impressed with Danny's effectiveness and efficiency. He asked if Danny would meet with him at the embassy in the morning. He met with Danny privately and thanked him for saving his life and protecting him and his family in such a skillful and professional manner. Along with his thanks, he gave Danny a check for $250,000. He also said that he would personally request that Danny provide security on all future visits for himself and his family, and other ministry officials as well.

That's when Danny got the idea to quit the force and start his own security agency. In fact, the first thing he did was to quit the police force. The second thing he did was to take the check. He wanted me to go in with him; I told him that I wasn't ready for that kind of move yet, but I offered to help him get the business up and running. I helped Danny set up the business structure and get a lot of the paperwork in place. I knew an attorney who took care of the legal stuff and licensing that was required. I spent much time with Danny and helped him a lot. There wasn't much marketing to do. The Sudan security business belonged to Danny. From that business came other business.

Things also changed for me in Washington, D.C. It happened a couple of years after I moved there. It was like a revelation, and I always wondered why it hadn't happened sooner. In Washington, D.C., Larry Stone accepted Larry Stone. Back in high school, I had never dated, until I met Ellen. I only saw Ellen. I only wanted to see Ellen. Before I met Ellen, I had always thought I needed to be like somebody else in order to be popular with girls. Even when I was with Ellen, I would have those thoughts sometimes. Like if I was James Bond or Magnum, PI, I would have it made. Appealing to and going out with women would be easy.

My life began to change when I met Ellen. She was my first girlfriend and I wanted to be with her all the time. We dated and went steady in our senior year in high school, and we stayed together all through college. After college, I enlisted in the Navy. Ellen and I were apart, and in time we became even more detached from each other. I started going out a little, and I found that it was enjoyable and not too difficult to do. When I moved to Washington, D.C., I started going out a lot. It was even more enjoyable, and now it was very easy to do. I realized that I'm myself, and that I am okay as myself. I don't have to look like or be like anyone else. Larry Stone accepted Larry Stone, and that was a revelation.

Another revelation was that many others accepted me also. I mean females accepted me, liked me, and liked to be with me. Believe it or not, and this was difficult for me to fathom, I was in demand. Dating became a very natural thing for me, and I went out a lot. In fact, I went out so much that relationships became easy to get into and to get out of as well. I found myself never fully opening up and giving one hundred percent to any of the relationships, and I began to think of many of the relationships as being meaningless.

Things were beginning to get confusing. A woman friend would spend the night at my house and then leave the next morning to go to her house. It was good company, good sex, and I didn't even have to leave my house. But there was something missing. There was no love, and that began to bother me a lot. Larry Stone accepting Larry Stone was wonderful. Women wanting Larry Stone was even more wonderful. But I wanted more. I wanted to be in love with someone, and I wanted that someone to be in love with me. That was the biggest revelation! I pined for true love and for that right woman to go through life with. I thought about Ellen.

Everything was clicking nicely at work until I got shot while trying to mediate a domestic dispute between a husband and wife. Under normal circumstances, I wouldn't even have been there, but we were short on personnel that night, and they asked if I would back-up one of the officers on this assignment. The neighbor who called in the disturbance mentioned that the wife had terminal cancer, and that she was in a lot of pain both physically and mentally. To make matters worse, her husband was cheating on her. When we arrived at their house, the woman had already shot and killed her husband. She was shaking and sobbing as she knelt over his body, the gun still clutched in her hand. And there in the middle of it all was her little girl, terrified and crying.

Before I had a chance to say anything, she pointed the gun at me and told us to stay back. I said that we would, and I asked her if there was anything I could do for her. She said that she would shoot her daughter and then kill herself, and that they'd both be better off dead together in peace than alive in misery and pain. I took my gun out of the holster and aimed it at her while she pointed her gun at me. In a calm and sincere voice, I asked her to please put the gun down. I told her that we could talk and work this out.

She said, "No! You don't understand! I won't be around to take care of my little girl. I want her to come with me!"

As she moved the gun away from me in the direction of her daughter, I screamed, "NO!!!!!" As I screamed, she shot me, and I shot her. I was hit in the right side of the chest. I was alive, but there was a lot of pain. The woman I shot was dead.

In the hospital, I experienced pain and sorrow. The physical pain from being shot paled in comparison to the mental anguish, suffering, and depression that I felt every time I thought about a little four-year-old girl who was now without a mom and dad, and alone in the world.

It took me back some twenty-five years to when I'd lost my own mom and dad. Remembering what happened then and how I had felt brought back the sadness. Now I felt that pain again, for my loss and for her loss. Because of me, she was now a little girl without a mother. What did she know now? What would she understand years from now? She was only four years old.

The police department worked aggressively with a number of city social service organizations, and a very nice woman who worked at one of the family service organizations adopted the girl. She had a son who was two. Now she had a little daughter who was four. I felt relieved that this little girl was with a loving family. But I also continued to feel guilty and depressed.

I didn't want to do much those days, just rest,

relax, and recuperate. I picked up a fourth R along the way—reading. I liked the mysteries the most. Maybe I could write one someday. I also enjoyed the movies. I saw most of the new releases, but the classics were my favorites. I really got a kick out of William Powell and Myrna Loy in the *Thin Man* series. Maybe I could write a book about a husband and wife who teamed up to solve mysteries or murders. It could be similar to the *Thin Man* series. I'd have to come up with some pretty good plots. A number of ideas were bouncing around in my head. My mind was finally mending. My body was also mending, and the hole in my chest was healing. Although I was operating on one lung, the doctor told me that I'd be able to do anything I wanted to with one healthy lung that I could have done with two. He also said that it was possible for the other lung to heal in time. For now, I'd just have to rest, start an exercise program, and get strong again.

The psychologist that was designated by the police department met with me once a week to help me understand my feelings about what had happened. At first I felt very guilty and angry, thinking that it was my fault that an innocent child was without her mother and would never see her mother again. I had shot and killed this child's mother. I learned to understand that it was not my fault, that I had not caused it to happen. I was also told that had I not been there, an innocent little child might also be dead. It all made sense when it was spoken and when I heard it, but it was hard to accept and live with. But I was learning to accept and live with it. I was made to see that it was important to go on with life, and that life should never be taken for granted. One must live in the present, and plan for the future. It was more important to try to make things better for today and tomorrow than to live in the sadness of the past. I also learned that it was okay to visit the past, to experience the good and loving memories of the past, and to be happy for them. Or to briefly visit the bad memories of the past and feel sad about them, but not to stay in the past, just visit. My body and mind were healing, and I was becoming healthy. I started exercising regularly, and I began to feel stronger. I started thinking positively, and I began to feel better. Recuperation was progressing nicely.

21

While I was recuperating, Mom and Dad would call me from Duluth at least once a month to see how I was doing. Before that we had spoken to each other less frequently. Sometimes only Mom would call and talk to me. I think she was worried about me. They both loved me, but Mom was the worrier. I wasn't much of a talker, so our conversations were brief. I'd hear from Linda every once in a while. She was married now and busy with a family of her own.

Randy and I spoke to each other every other week. We had a regular routine, in which he would call, then I would call, and so on and so forth. It seemed that Randy and I had the most to say to each other. Randy was married also, and he took over running All Duluth Realty after Ruby retired. Ruby would still come in about once a week, and sell a house now and then, and also consult on architectural projects once in a while. But for the most part Ruby was retired and didn't want to have anything to do with running All Duluth Realty. Randy would tell me that Ruby viewed All Duluth Realty like a grandchild now. He liked to play with it a little, enjoy it, but let someone else take care of it.

Randy and I talked about a lot of things. But

we never spoke about Ellen. Our conversations were mostly about real estate. Randy would tell me about office buildings that were being developed, new homes that were being built, what the buildings and houses were selling for, what commissions he was getting, and the competition. He would go on and on. And the more he told me, the more questions I had, and the more I wanted to know. I enjoyed our talks, especially the real estate gossip, and my mind became alert and alive with the business of real estate. Randy always sent me the Sunday *Duluth News Tribune* by express mail so I'd have it by Tuesday at the latest. Sometimes he would get an early edition of the Sunday paper on Saturday and send it to me, so I'd have it by Monday. Once or twice during our talks, we spoke about a visit, he here or I there. During our last conversation, he said that it would be better for me to come to Duluth, so that I could see the whole family. They all missed me, especially Mom and Dad.

I said, "I'll be ready to visit soon. We'll talk about it again."

He said, "Are you just saying that or are you meaning that?"

I said, "No, I've been thinking about visiting, I really mean it. We'll talk again soon."

22

I was quite surprised when Randy showed up on my doorstep in Vienna, Virginia, one Saturday morning in September 1983. It seemed that nearly everyone who worked in Washington, D.C., lived either in Maryland or Virginia. With a big grin on his face, he looked at me, nodded his head approvingly, and said, "Hello, Larry. I'm here to see how you're doing. We have spoken a lot, but I wanted to see for myself. You look fine."

"Randy, I can't believe you're here in Virginia!" We hugged. "Come on in. Sit down. Relax. Yes, I'm fine, feel good, getting stronger every day."

Randy sat down. He stared at me and smiled. Then he said, "Strong enough to come to Duluth, Larry? You know Mom and Dad have not seen you for a long time. They miss you and they worry about you a lot. We all miss you."

As Randy's words sank in, I realized that I had been disconnected from my family for more than ten years. That made me feel melancholy, and in a subdued voice I said, "I miss all of you too, and I was thinking about visiting sometime soon."

Randy was very serious now, and his eyes searched mine as he replied, "I'm not talking about a visit, I'm talking about coming home. Do you ever think about moving back to Duluth?"

"It's too soon to think that far ahead, Randy. I'm not sure where I'll settle down, down the road, or what I'll do either."

Randy continued, "Look, Larry, with all the real estate we've been talking, you probably know more about selling real estate in Duluth now than you did when you were there. Why not come home? You and I can run All Duluth Realty together, both of us as broker-owners and partners."

I was surprised and happy at the offer, and I expressed my happiness as I replied, "That's really nice, Randy, and generous, and I appreciate the offer. But what does Ruby say?"

Randy replied, "He really misses you a lot, Larry. He always wanted both of us to run the business. As a matter of fact, he said I should just come down here, pick you up, and bring you back."

I could picture Ruby telling Randy to go to D.C., just pick Larry up, and bring him back to Duluth. I briefly thought about that image, smiled, and said, "I miss him too. And Melanie. And you and Linda. But I'm not sure I'm ready to return to Duluth just yet. Besides, you're running the business now, and I'm sure you're doing a great job. You don't need me there."

"Ah, that's where you're wrong, Larry. I've got my hands full with doing the commercial real estate and new home development. I can't keep an eye on existing home sales. That was always your area of expertise. I think it still is. Together we could have that business really humming. Also, like I said, it was always Dad's dream to see both of us running the company, and the company doing the lion's share of Duluth's real estate business."

"Let's talk about this later, Randy. Have you had breakfast yet? No? Okay. I know a great Virginia inn that serves the best breakfast in town. It's out in the country a bit, real comfortable, good food, and pretty waitresses. We can eat, relax, and you can tell me everything that's going on in Duluth."

Randy and I drove out to the Sir Walter Raleigh Inn, and we settled into a large, comfortable booth in a small dining room that we had all to ourselves. We ordered a sumptuous breakfast. Randy had the Belgian waffles and eggs combo, while I opted for steak and a cheese omelet. Usually we were both fast eaters, but this morning, we were men of leisure. Randy filled me in on what was happening in Duluth, not just in real estate, but the changes that were going on, new faces, old faces, people, and places. We talked about the Duluth mansions on London Road, and the other great Duluth houses. Randy paused for a moment or two and then said, "How would you like to sell one of those big houses, Larry?"

I nodded my head in agreement; "I'd really like that, Randy. Yes, that would be something!"

Randy looked into my eyes. The smile that had been there before left his face. He now looked very sad. Slowly, he said, "I saw Ellen Sommers, used to be Ellen Westphal, a couple of weeks ago with her lovely little daughter, Jane. You know, Jane just turned eight. What a lovely little lady."

"Ellen Westphal, I mean Ellen Sommers," I said wistfully. "I'll tell you something, Randy. I always regretted not being able to commit to Ellen when we went to college. I sensed that she was ready to get married, but I knew that I wasn't. I should have been, because Ellen was very special to me. You know, I really loved her. More than she knew, I think, and much more than I knew. How is she doing?"

Very slowly, Randy replied, "Ellen had a terrible tragedy in her life, Larry."

"What happened? Is she okay?" I was nervous and my heartbeat increased rapidly as the questions left my lips.

"Well, Ellen lost her husband, Jim, about six months ago. It was heartbreaking for her and Jane. The family was very close. It was an automobile accident. No reason why it happened. It just happened. Jim was driving home from work, late one evening, and his car went off the road, down a steep ravine. It caught fire and then exploded. It was an awful accident. Ellen had to identify the body, or what was left of it. Linda was at the funeral. There was a lot of sadness and a lot of tears."

Randy continued, "Now they seem to be recovering, Ellen and Jane. I always see them together. The way they love each other and support each other, it's wonderful to see. They are both brave and strong, mother and daughter and best friends." Randy stopped. He must have seen the sadness in my eyes and sensed the pain that I felt inside me. He gently put his hand on my shoulder and asked, "Are you okay, Larry?"

In a troublous tone of voice, I replied, "Yeah, I'm okay. But I feel sad for Ellen and Jane and I'm also angry. I just don't understand it. Poor Ellen. Such a good person. She didn't deserve that. I don't understand how something like that could happen. I sometimes wonder why God lets bad things happen to good people. What kind of God lets things like that happen?"

Randy looked at me. He rubbed his eyes and slowly shook his head. "There's no explanation, Larry. I don't believe that God wants these things to happen. They just happen. Life has to go on. People have to keep living. And people help people through bad times. That's where God comes in, Larry."

We sat in silence for a few minutes. Then Randy spoke, "If you don't mind me changing the subject, you know that mansion on London Road, 'Bedford House,' the big one overlooking the lake? It's the one with twenty-six rooms, six fireplaces, and a separate carriage house. It sits on a hill and it has stunning views of the lake and the shoreline. It's going to be put up for sale in a few months. And the owners have already signed a listing agreement with Duluth's favorite real estate company, All Duluth Realty. They want us to present the home as an historic landmark, one of the Zenith City's most prestigious mansions. They also would like it to remain as a single-family residence. And they want it to go on the market in December. I told them, 'No problem. We'll have everything completed by the end of November and have the place on the market in December.' Maybe it will sell before Christmas!"

"Hey Randy, that's a pretty big deal. What a great house to sell. It's definitely not your office building type deal, is it? Will you be able to handle it?"

"I'm pretty sure I can handle it, but I do have some concerns. Just between you and me, Larry, I don't think I can give it the treatment that it deserves. But you could do it, Larry. You could do it for sure! I wouldn't trust it to anyone else. It's more than just a house, much more. It's a big part of Duluth's history. It's got to be handled and marketed in a special way. It would be a great 'welcome back to Duluth' first listing for you, Larry. It's yours with no strings attached. Come back to Duluth and take care of it."

23

Over the past eleven years, I've visited Duluth now and then to see Ruby, Melanie, Randy, and Linda. I'd only stay for short periods of time. Two days here, three days there—quick visits to Duluth and then back to my job and my life in Washington, D.C. Now after recuperating for about a year in D.C., I'm actually thinking about going back to Duluth for an extended period of time. Who knows, maybe for a long time. Maybe I'll settle down and live and work in Duluth. It'll be good to see Mom, Dad, Randy, and Linda on a regular basis.

Who am I kidding? What I'm really thinking about is seeing Ellen after all these years. Ellen and her daughter. I never saw them when I visited in the past. Ellen had her own life, so I blocked her out of my life. She would come to visit my brain now and then, and when she did, I would think of how things might have been for us. I would also think about how things used to be. Sweet and sentimental daydreams. They'd come and then they'd go. They'd make me feel happy, but they'd also make me feel sad. For the most part, I put Ellen and everything about Ellen out of my mind. I had always been good at walking away from things and putting them out of my mind when I wanted to. But I don't want to now. I want to know how Ellen is doing and how she feels about me now. I want to know how she will react when she hears my voice and when she sees me. I want to know how I will feel when I talk to her and when I see her.

Although my body is standing still, my mind is moving at warp speed. Soon I'll be in Duluth. The first thing I should do is to find a place to stay. The first thing I will do is to call Ellen. Then I'll arrange to ship my car and my other personal possessions to Duluth. There won't be a lot to ship. I sold my house in D.C. and most of the furniture with it. Whatever happens in Duluth, I have no plans to return to D.C. That part of my life is over. I don't want to live there anymore. I'll rent for six months first. That should give me enough time to see if things are working out, and if they are, then I'll find a house to buy. I have to buy something within two years; otherwise all the money I make on the sale of my D.C. house will be taxed as capital gains. I can't have that. I've got to throw it into a Duluth house that will cost the same or more than the house I sold in D.C. Then I'll have no taxes to pay. That's kind of a stupid tax law. They should change it. Suppose someone is downsizing or lost their job or something like that. It would make more sense to say, whatever the amount of their gain, that they would have to buy a house for at least that amount, in order to avoid paying capital gains tax. Or if they lived in their home for the past three years or more, there'd be no tax on the gain regardless of whether they purchased another house or not. That would make much more sense.

My place in D.C. sold for $195,000. Let's see, a $195,000 plus house in Duluth, that should be some house, maybe a "castle" with a view of the lake. I always loved looking at the lake. Maybe this is my chance to get something with a view of the lake. Or lakeshore—that would be something! I hope that Lake Superior looks as beautiful and blue as I remember it from years past. For now though, I'll find a house to rent, something away from it all. Maybe close to the lake. I'd like that. I better get a second car; I mean truck, to deal with the Duluth winters. It wouldn't do to take my Jaguar out for a spin in the snow. Maybe a Chevy Blazer with four-wheel drive. That would work out well.

The newspapers were always a good source for rental homes. I'll check out the *Duluth News Tribune*, and see what's available. I'll also put out some feelers to the real estate companies and agents in case they know of any houses for rent. I might as well let the rental agents know what I'm looking for.

I'd like a house with great views. Two bedrooms on the same level would be nice, and another downstairs for company. I'd have to have a garage for two cars. I also want to have at least one wood-burning fireplace in a family room or a great room of sorts. That would keep me warm during those deep-freeze Duluth winters. I always wanted a fireplace in the master bedroom as well. That might be hard to find. But I could always put one in. And I'd want central air-conditioning for the summers. I'm definitely getting weather-wimpy and much more comfort-minded in my older years. I'd need to have two baths, one on each level, and a nice gently sloping lot overlooking the lake would be just perfect. Maybe an acre. But not less than three-quarters of an acre. Whoa, what am I thinking about! Slow down, Stone! You're only renting, not buying. It's so easy for me to get carried away when I'm thinking about houses. But if I were buying, wouldn't it be nice to have one of those historic stately mansions? Maybe a smaller one with ten rooms instead of thirty. And a view of the lake. I can't forget about the lake!

When I return to Duluth, I'll become a broker-owner of All Duluth Realty and a partner. Randy and I will own and run the brokerage. Randy will be involved in commercial real estate, and new home development and construction. I will be involved in listing houses and selling houses, and in locating buyers for all houses that are available for sale. Randy always admired my affinity for the hogger, and my ability to hog, and he always said I had the best record around when it came to hogging. Getting a hogger would ensure that you'd get both sides of the commission. For most agents, hogging was a once in a while occurrence. For me, it was a solid 15 percent of the time occurrence. At least that's what it used to be.

It was just like Randy had said. When I returned to Duluth in the beginning of October, there were two owners of All Duluth Realty, Randy and myself. Randy was in charge of the commercial real estate and the new home construction. I was in charge of residential real estate sales. We each had a nice office, and we were responsible for promoting business in our specific market areas and for providing supervision and oversight to our respective agents.

All Duluth Realty was a medium-sized company with nine employees, three of whom were involved in commercial real estate and new home development. Four others handled residential sales, and two others provided administrative support and did closings as well. Ruby had a nice office also. He'd sell a house every once in a while or consult on a commercial deal, but I was told that if we saw him more than once a week, that was a lot. Randy explained that we'd have our sales meetings once a week, every Tuesday or Wednesday morning. It sounded good to me.

All Duluth Realty was a full-service brokerage, very customer-oriented, with competitive and flexible rates. While most of our customers opted for a 6 percent commission rate, there were times when the rate was less. When the rate was less, the homeowner would pick up some of the sales and marketing efforts. Sometimes a seller might try to sell their home on their own. We would be there to assist with the paperwork and to conduct the closing. On rare occasions the commission rate might be more than 6 percent. When this happened, and Ruby got wind of it, he would start muttering something about three wise men appearing from the East. However, the truth of the matter was that when the commission rate was more, the brokerage would perform some enhanced marketing and promotional duties above and beyond the full-service that was normally provided. Additionally, an agent could offer a lower rate for hoggers. That might give the agent an edge in getting the listing. Most agents never discussed reducing the commission under any circumstances. However, I always made it clear to my clients that the commission would be reduced if I listed and sold the home. It became part of my listing presentation, and I would write it into the listing contract. It gave me a competitive edge, especially since my hogger rate was still 15 percent. I was also considering an even lower rate if the seller brought in the buyer. I could qualify the buyer, write up the purchase agreement, complete any additional paperwork, and coordinate the closing. I liked the idea of my sellers competing with me.

BROKER'S OPEN

As I had promised myself, the first thing I did when I got to Duluth was to call Ellen. I couldn't stop thinking about her, and I wanted to let her know that I was here. I started to call and then stopped. I got nervous, because I hadn't spoken to her for so long and I didn't know how she would react to my call. It was in the evening when I arrived in Duluth, and I was thinking, "Maybe it is too late to call now. Maybe I should call her in the morning instead." It was weird. It was like deja vu, like high school all over again. I was thinking of excuses not to call.

I said to myself, "Enough of this!" and I made the call. We spoke for about two hours, and I remembered how easy it was to talk to Ellen. We talked about the good things in our lives and the bad things that had happened to us over the past years. We talked and listened and talked some more. It was all so natural, the words flowing freely, the strong feelings and the sincere thoughts—our openness and our honesty. I felt that I could talk to Ellen about anything, and I think she felt the same way with me. And in those two hours, I think we spoke about most everything that was important to us.

I said, "I'd like to see you and Jane. Could I take you both out to lunch somewhere, to one of your favorite restaurants?"

"Yes, that would be very nice, Larry. When?"

"How about tomorrow, Saturday. Is that too soon?"

"No, that's good."

"Great, I'll pick you both up about noon. What kind of food does Jane like?"

"She's pretty easy when it comes to food."

"Does she like pizza?"

"She loves it, and so do I."

"I know you do. I'll see you both tomorrow around noon."

24

They were both in front of their house when I drove up. I got out of the black Jaguar and walked over to them. Ellen was as beautiful as I remembered. As a matter of fact, she looked stunning. She smiled, and as I held out my hand to shake hands, she gave me a hello hug, and then introduced her daughter, Jane. I looked at Jane and held out my hand again, and Jane took it, shook it, and said hello. She had a good grip for a little kid. She was very pretty, with a lovely smile on a happy face and a sparkle in her eyes. She looked past me and asked, "What's that animal?"

I turned, saw nothing, and asked, "What animal?"

She giggled, pointed to the front of my car, and said, "That animal. The one on top of your car."

The three of us walked to the front of the car, and there, sure enough, we were face to face with a sleek silver jaguar that stared back at us. "That's a jaguar, Jane, a big jungle cat."

"I know that, but why is it there on your car?"

"That's the kind of car it is, Jane. It's a Jaguar. The company that built the car put the jaguar there so that everyone would know it's a

Jaguar car."

"Why did they call a car a Jaguar?"

"I think they felt that since the car was black and sleek and fast like a jaguar, they might as well call it a Jaguar."

Jane and the jaguar were locked in an eye-to-eye stare and neither one of them was backing down. Ellen, although amused by Jane's curiosity, suggested that we all get in the car and go for lunch. Jane asked if she could touch the jaguar. I said yes. She did, the trance was broken, and the three of us went to lunch.

We went to Grandma's Saloon & Deli in downtown Duluth. The food was delicious. Both Ellen and Jane had hearty appetites, and we enjoyed a nice leisurely lunch and some dessert brownies as well. We then drove around a bit, took a walk by the lake, and I got them back home at about 4:30 p.m. It was a perfect afternoon. Ellen thanked me for lunch and for a delightful afternoon, and so did Jane. Jane gave the jaguar a good-bye look and stare. Ellen gave me another hug and said, "It's great to see you. Call me later, after eight tonight. Okay?"

I said, "I will." I waved good-bye, drove away, and thought about our first kiss in high school. And the many kisses after that. I remembered the first time we made love. How our bodies fit together perfectly. Well, almost perfectly. How we held each other, the pleasure and excitement of our bodies touching, and how we trembled in ecstasy in the heat of love. It was beginning to get hot inside the car.

I stopped at a gasoline station for some cold water to drink and to splash on my face. That felt much better. I found a phone and called the Jaguar dealer in Duluth. I spoke to the manager and then to a person in the parts department and ordered a sleek silver jaguar, just like the one that stood on top of the hood of my car. They had a couple in stock, so I drove over to pick one up before the dealership closed.

That night I called Ellen at 8:30. She said that they had had a wonderful afternoon and that Jane liked me. She added that it was good to see me again. She mentioned that I looked fit and trim and wondered if I was working out. I said that I had been playing a lot of tennis, doing push-ups and sit-ups, and working out a little before I got shot. I had taken a hiatus during recuperation, and I'd been getting back into exercising over the past several months.

I told her that she looked great and that Jane was adorable, a real little sweetheart.

She said, "Yes, that's my little Jane. Eight and going on eighteen! She worries about me and watches over me." She paused shortly, then said, "Listen, Larry. Would you like to come over tomorrow for a home-cooked meal? Let's say dinner, sometime between six and six-thirty. I'm making turkey with stuffing, and Jane's helping."

"That sounds great, Ellen. I'd really like that. I

have a little gift for Jane. Is there anything that I can bring?"

"No, Larry. Just bring yourself. See you tomorrow then."

It was hard to fall asleep that night. I kept thinking about Ellen. When I finally did fall asleep, Ellen visited me in my dreams. I remember trying to put my arms around her, but she kept slipping away. I finally got hold of her, and just as we were about to kiss I woke up.

In the morning, I thought about that dream. I couldn't figure it out, so I ignored it, and it went away. I thought about this evening instead. I thought about Ellen and Jane. I'll give Jane that jaguar tonight. I'll also pick up a gift for Ellen. I know what I'll get for her, the movie *Paris Blues*. A movie for Ellen, a jaguar for Jane, and a bottle of wine to go with dinner. I'd better pick up a fruit juice for Jane also.

25

I arrived at Ellen's place a little after six. I hadn't eaten much during the day, and I was ready for some turkey and stuffing. And I could hardly wait to see Ellen again. I brought a bottle of white wine and a fancy strawberry fruit juice for Jane. Jane was very observant and noticed the medium-sized box that was wrapped with blue sparkling paper on the sofa. It was something new that hadn't been there before, and it had captured her attention. She pointed to the box and said, "What's that, Mom?"

"Oh, that. That's something Larry brought for you."

"What is it?"

"I have no idea what it could be. I think it's a surprise for you. So we won't know until you open it."

"Can I open it now?"

"Right after dinner you can open it, just before dessert. Okay?"

"Okay, Mom."

During dinner and in between talking and staring at the box, Jane told us about her adventures at school. Unlike many pre-teens, Jane was an organizational whiz. She wrote the activities for the upcoming week on a calendar chalkboard. She was eager to share them with us. She went through the Monday routine at school in great detail, and then gave us a stirring synopsis of what the rest of the week would be like. By the time we were finishing dinner, Jane had brought Ellen and me up-to-date on next week's planned activities. She was now gazing intently at the blue box. Ellen said, "Well, Jane, are you going to open it?"

In a split second or less, Jane had the box in her hand and was studying it from all angles. She then began unwrapping it very carefully, so carefully, in fact, that the fancy wrapping paper was hardly disturbed. After a long and laborious process, Jane began opening the box, and a look of surprise and delight danced across her face. She retrieved the prize and held it up proudly for us to see. There was the same sleek, silver jaguar that she had seen on my car's hood the day before, now safe and secure in her firm grasp.

Jane's face lit up with excitement and happiness. She let out with a couple of excited "Wows!" Ellen was also surprised, and echoed Jane with a "Wow! What a wonderful gift! What do you say, Jane?"

"Thank you, Larry, it's so shiny and beautiful. But how about your car? Doesn't it need to stay there so that people will know it's a Jaguar car?"

"Oh, that's okay, Jane. The car still has its jaguar, and now you have one also. Two identical sleek, silver jaguars—one for my car and the other one for you."

"Thanks again, Larry."

"You're welcome, Jane."

Ellen said, "Okay you two, let's all have some dessert. After dessert it's time to get your stuff ready for school and then off to bed, Jane."

"Mom, can I take the jaguar to school tomorrow for show and tell?"

"Yes, you can, Jane, but don't lose it."

"Don't worry, Mom. I won't."

"Okay, Jane, dessert time. And then get ready for bed. When you're ready, I'll tuck you in."

As Jane got ready for bed, I said, "Here's a little something I got for you, Ellen." Ellen opened her gift and there were Paul Newman, Sidney Poitier, Joanne Woodward, and Diahann Carroll staring her in the face from the cover of the video of *Paris Blues*, our first movie together.

"This is wonderful and very thoughtful too. You're still a sentimental romantic, aren't you, and that's just one of the things I really like about you. I'll go tuck Jane in and be right down."

When Ellen returned, she looked at the video jacket and said she hadn't seen that movie since we'd seen it together in high school. She smiled and said, "We'll have to watch it again one day."

I said, "I'd like that."

We sat on the sofa, held hands, and talked about our feelings and things that were important to us. About our jobs, our homes, our lives, and our families. Ellen talked about her daughter.

I listened. She smiled with happy tears in her eyes when she talked about Jane. I held her close to me and smiled stoically, but my eyes were becoming cloudy and misty too. Ellen noticed. She took my hand, stood up, and started walking. I held her hand and followed.

In her bedroom we held each other gently but firmly, not wanting to lose each other ever again. She asked if this was right. I said yes. We kissed and touched, and enjoyed the excitement of first love, lost love, and love found. Our passion was a slow burn. Like a good fire in a fireplace, whose heat and warmth lingered through the night. We made love tenderly and thoroughly. My body tingled and trembled all over, in complete ecstasy. A melting of body and mind in pure pleasure and total satisfaction. I hoped she felt the same as I did. I said, "That was delicious."

She said, "The best!" We continued to hold each other.

After a while I said, "Ellen, I want to stay here, and wake up in the morning with you in my arms, and kiss you as the sun rises. But I'm thinking of Jane, and I want the timing to be right and to do the right thing by all of us."

Ellen looked at me and said, "The timing is right for me, Larry. I'd love to wake up in the morning with your arms around me. But I know what you're saying and I appreciate your thoughtfulness. I also want it to be right for the three of us too." Enough talking.

BROKER'S OPEN

We caressed each other and came together again before the sun kissed the moon and splashed the sky with early morning light. And then I left.

26

I delivered the "People who hate Stone" list to Detective June Brown, and we spent some time going over it and talking about it. I categorized the names chronologically, looking at specific periods of time, and then fitting people and places into those respective time slots.

I reviewed the list with Detective Brown and provided additional detail that I thought would be of value. I tried to include everything; I had no intention of leaving anything out.

I felt like a storyteller as I began speaking, "From 1958 to 1962, I attended East High School. Big Howie (Howard Simkey) hated my guts. I think he hated me because I was Jewish. I wasn't afraid to stand up to him and I hurt him badly once. I'm sure that chess opponents and tennis opponents probably didn't like me much either. I played a lot of chess in my first three years of high school. I was a very tough competitor and I always played with a passion to win. Winning was more important to me than anything else. From 1962 to 1966, I attended the University of Minnesota and sold real estate. I didn't play much chess then, maybe a game once in a while. However, I did sell a lot of real estate. I was a real 'go-getter' and extremely competitive. I suppose

120

that other real estate agents who objected to my New York competitiveness might easily have hated me. During college, Ellen and I were still going together. Any Ellen admirers could have easily hated me. From 1966 to 1970 I was in the Navy. There were no Stone haters there, that I know of. From 1970 to 1972, I attended graduate school at the University of Minnesota and sold a lot of real estate. Again, other real estate agents may not have appreciated my overly aggressive, competitive style. From 1972 to 1982, I worked for the Washington, D.C., Metropolitan Police Department as a police psychologist and later as a detective in homicide. I left as a lieutenant. I'm sure that anyone I sent away hated me. There were also one or two co-workers who did not like me, and whom I did not like either. But they'd want me to stay in Duluth, not leave Duluth. During 1983 I was recuperating after being shot. I shot a woman and she died. She had shot her husband and was about to shoot her daughter. Even though it was in self-defense, I'm sure her family hates me. After that incident, I was put on involuntary disability retirement.

"It's not a great list of leads, June. Normally, I'm a low-key, live-and-let-live type of person. Sometimes, though, I can get aggressive. Now, Howie and I didn't get along from the first time we met. He called me a goddamn Jew and punched me and kicked me during what should have been a fun football game between neighborhood kids.

Larry Stoller

After the game, he tried to beat me up some more. I put a rock to his head, and since then we've both stayed out of each other's way. During high school, I was on the tennis team. My form stunk, but I was a fierce competitor who never gave up. I've got to believe I might have rubbed some players the wrong way with my aggressive courtside behavior. I was also captain of the chess team. I beat everyone I played in high school and statewide tournaments. I wasn't really cocky, but I was proud, and sometimes flaunted it. I always played to win and to destroy my opponents, a nasty combination of chess-playing ability and psychological warfare. I must have ticked off the opposition at one time or another. I was also a bit tough with the team, ensuring that our strategy gave us the competitive advantage whenever we had team play. I suppose some of the guys might have been unhappy with me, but we won the state championship, so they could not have been too unhappy. In college, I didn't have much time to take part in extra-curricular activities. I played a little chess to keep myself mentally tough and I played some tennis for exercise. But I wasn't as crazy about winning as I'd been in high school. I also sold a lot of real estate. I'd have to admit that I was still very competitive when it came to selling. There could have been some real estate agents that I beat out of a listing or two. As I mentioned before, I saw Ellen all through college. I loved being with Ellen.

When we were together, life was wonderful, and everything around me seemed to be in harmony. Just thinking of her made me feel at peace with the world. It's possible that there might have been some Ellen admirers that did not like me around, but if there were, I didn't notice them."

I continued, "There were no problems in the Navy. I was in Naval Intelligence. We collected and analyzed information. We also conducted audits and investigations. It was a lot different than your typical Seabee life. I came back to Duluth after my hitch was up, went to graduate school, and sold real estate again. I kind of lost touch with Ellen while I was in the Service. When I returned to Duluth, she was doing an internship in Washington, D.C., so I jumped into selling real estate big time, while attending graduate school. Again, I could have rubbed some realtors the wrong way. But there were no incidents. Then, when Ellen was getting ready to come back to Duluth, I found out that she had become engaged in Washington, D.C., and would be married in Duluth when she returned with her fiancé. I didn't want to deal with that, so I took that police job in D.C. I'm sure there must have been some people that hated me there. I got shot there. Then I went on permanent disability retirement. I got a lot of rest and relaxation while I was recuperating, and I pretty much kept to myself. I returned to Duluth in October of 1983 and joined All Duluth Realty as a broker-owner and firm partner. I started seeing Ellen again. Her husband had died in an automobile accident. Then I listed the prestigious Bedford House. That must have been a loud wake-up call to some Duluth realtors. Then Sherry Stensgard holds the broker's open instead of me, and she's brutally murdered, and we're in the middle of this living nightmare. I also listed a nice contemporary home a few days after I listed Bedford House. I think that's pretty much it, June."

June nodded her head, "Thanks, Larry. That's good information, and it will be valuable to us in our investigation. I know all of this is not easy for you." She paused for a moment and then asked, "What are your plans now?"

"I've been doing some thinking, June, and I know that I can't sell any real estate here in Duluth with this psycho on the loose. To tell you the truth, June, I don't think I can stay here or live here either. I'm thinking that I should leave, maybe go back to Washington or go somewhere else. It might be better for everyone here for me not to be here."

June looked at me skeptically and said, "You don't really believe that, do you, Larry?"

"Well, I'm not sure what to believe, June. Under the circumstances, there's no way I'm going to sell houses here and put anybody else at risk. So real estate in Duluth is out of the question. And I'm thinking that even staying here in Duluth could put people in harm's way. I can't allow that to happen. On the other hand, I'd like to stay and help catch this sick son of a bitch."

"Listen to me, Larry. What happened wasn't your fault. It happened, and somewhere out there is a murderer with a twisted mind and a twisted reason for doing what he did. We don't know the reason, and we don't know if he'll do it again, whether you're here or not. So we have to find him and stop him, so that 'worse will not happen.' You were a police psychologist, a detective and a pretty good one, I'm told. You can help us get this animal by working with us." June's clear brown eyes now grew large and bright. They were like incandescent cat eyes that beckoned me to gaze upon their light. As I gazed at the glowing light, I heard June softly say, "So you can't leave here until this is resolved, and things are made right. You know that's how it has to be, Larry."

Almost automatically, and in a voice void of expression, I replied, "You're right, June. I can't walk away from this one. I can't even run away. There's too much at stake here. Not just my life, but the lives of others too. I love Ellen, and I won't lose her again. And Sherry Stensgard's senseless death. And a madman who's still out there somewhere and threatening that 'worse will happen.' I have to stay here and see this thing through. I'll do whatever I can to help."

27

The Bedford House murder was a hot potato and right up there on the top of Detective June Brown's list of unsolved homicides. The heat from the mayor's office was cranked up high. It made the Duluth deep-freeze feel like a Miami heat wave, especially at Duluth Police Headquarters, where the temperatures reached record highs. The heat from City Hall was fueled by a number of *Duluth News Tribune* articles about safety precautions that real estate agents should take when conducting open houses. The newspaper reminded its readers that the Bedford Murderer was still at large and that Duluth realtors were not safe. The Duluth Association of Realtors was on the mayor's case to get results. June Brown and her detectives interviewed all of the 49 brokers and 323 realtors in Duluth. The kind of questions they asked were: "Did you hear about the murder at Bedford House? How did you hear about it? Did you know about the Bedford House broker's open? How did you hear about it? Did you let your agents know about the broker's open? Did you pass out information about the broker's open to your agents? When did you first hear about the murder there? Did you know Sherry Stensgard? Did you know Larry Stone?

Did you compete for the Bedford House listing?
Do you know anything at all that might help us in
this case?"

While the questions asked were always the
same, the answers received were not. For
example, a number of brokers and realtors knew
of Larry Stone—many others did not. The
detectives recorded the answers received and they
paid careful attention to the manner and tone in
which questions were answered. The question
"Did you know Larry Stone?" was a favorite of
theirs. They carefully recorded all the answers,
and included notes about non-verbal expressions
and/or responses that they observed or heard.
With a total of 372 interviews, there was a lot of
information recorded. However, no leads were
identified from the interviews.

The detectives did learn that three other real
estate brokers had competed for the Bedford
House listing. They also discovered that sixteen
brokers and/or realtors stated that they had gone
to the Bedford House broker's open. They had all
been turned away by the police, with the
exception of the first broker who arrived and
found the body, and called the police. That broker
was instructed to remain in the house without
touching anything, prevent others from entering
the house by locking the front door, and wait
until the police arrived.

Additionally, the detectives interviewed people
in the neighborhood of Bedford House. The only

information that came out of the neighborhood interviews was that one woman had noticed a car driving into the Bedford House driveway the day before, a little past the noon hour. She described it as a fancy black car. It was confirmed to be Larry Stone's car. Larry Stone and Sherry Stensgard had gone to Bedford House the day before the open house to discuss the house features.

The crime scene inspection and investigation indicated that entry into Bedford House had been through a rear door. The lock had been picked. Exit from the house was through the rear door as well. It was determined that the murderer entered the house in the evening or in the early morning while it was still dark, and rested until Sherry Stensgard arrived to prepare for the open house. There were indented cushions on a sofa and a chair that seemed out of place. There were also large footprints inside the house and by the rear house entrance, where the carpeting had been slightly soiled. But the carpet had been cleaned, in preparation for the open house, right before the owners had left to go abroad. The police also found strands of hair beside the victim. A lab analysis indicated that the hair was not human hair but synthetic hair.

28

After the murder at Bedford House, there was another incident. One of my other listings, a unique three-bedroom, three-bath contemporary split on the top of a hill in the Lakeside section of Duluth, was burned to the ground a few days after it was listed. That happened at the beginning of the third week in December—just before the holidays. There was hardly anything left to salvage. The owners were at their business when it happened, but their beautiful snow-white, three-year-old Samoyed perished in the flames. They had no children, and their dog was part of their family. They loved their dog, the way parents would love their child. Their grief was overwhelming.

At the time of the fire there was a dusting of snow. A thin white blanket of new snow covered the ground. The neighbors next door called the fire department. They also called the owners and me. I got there quickly. It was a strange sight, this combination of white snow, orange and yellow flames, and black and gray smoke—hot and cold together on a frigid winter day.

With new snow on the ground, some clues were uncovered and shared with me by Detective

June Brown. There were footprints—shoe prints might be a better description—found in the snow in back of the house. They were big prints, too, probably a size 13, a different size than those of the firemen, and different treads also. There were a number of these footprints found around the house. There was also the smell of gasoline and some gasoline spills in the snow. This was no accident. This was a planned and premeditated burn. A fast and furious fire. It was the work of a deranged someone who hated me and wanted me to disappear from Duluth. Why not just go after me? Do the job right and get rid of me. Did this someone want to see me suffer and be in pain? And it didn't matter who was killed, or who got hurt, or what was destroyed, as long as what happened could be tied to my being in Duluth? But why get rid of me because I'm selling real estate? Or because of my marketing methods? Or because of my religious background? No, there had to be more to it. But what? What was this someone afraid of? Was I taking away his livelihood, his power, his position? Or was it something else?

The day after the fire, I received a note at the real estate office in the mail. It was on a plain white sheet of paper inside a plain white envelope. Written on the paper were the words "LEAVE DULUTH JEW."

There were now two incidents in less than two weeks, and I had received the same kind of message in both instances. I was sure that it was the work of the same person, but it was not the same workmanship. The Bedford House murder was carried out meticulously and the police were without a clue. The house burning was messy and the police had a preponderance of sharply pointed clues. This disconnect was very disturbing. I was unable to attach a handle to it. As I thought more about it, an uneasy and unsettling feeling pitted the inside of my gut. It suggested that there was much more going on here than real estate and religion, and that neither the police nor I had the faintest idea of what it was.

29

Based upon the hate list that I provided to Detective June Brown and the clues from my burned-down listing in Lakeside, she felt it was time to lean on Big Howie. After high school, Big Howie had gone into the remodeling business and the landscaping business as well. A review of records and receipts for maintenance work performed at Bedford House indicated that some landscaping projects were completed by The Evergreen Company in May 1983. These projects included rock and plant gardens in front and repairs to the brick walkways in the rear of the house. Evergreen was owned by Howard Simkey and managed by Renee Lilholtz.

The company didn't do much business until Renee Lilholtz was hired to manage it. She promoted the business and transformed it into a going concern. Renee was trained as a landscape architect and she had a good head for business. Through aggressive marketing and excellent customer relations, she was able to pick up some very good accounts and some significant business. Before long, she bought into the business, and she and Howie became partners. She tried to keep Howie away from the business as much as possible, as he had a way of antagonizing customers. She wanted him to be a silent partner—completely silent!

Detective June Brown had a number of questions that needed answers, and she would have Howard Simkey brought in for questioning. He had been interviewed once before, but that was a routine interview with companies that had done business at Bedford House over the past year or two. It was the same type of interview that was conducted with the brokers and realtors. However, with the discovery of new evidence from the house that was burned down, it was time to interview Big Howie again. This time, the detectives would ask pointed questions—about footprints, shoe treads, gas tanks, and gas smells. It would be a more grueling interview for Howard Simkey. The detectives would also want to know where he had been on certain dates at certain times.

I agreed with Detective June Brown. Bring him in right away, throw him on the grill, turn up the heat, and see what happens. However, I had another idea. I would check him out myself.

Howard Simkey also owned Precision Home Remodeling, a company that specialized in light construction and renovating projects. I had called Evergreen Company and had spoken to Renee Lilholtz. She told me that Howard could be found at the construction company, not at the landscaping business. Renee didn't want him around, bothering the workers and scaring away the customers. Since she was running Evergreen, a part owner, and bringing in the bucks, he stayed away. She also suggested that when he was not at the construction company, he could be found at a downtown Duluth bar called the Real Duluth Grill.

The new evidence pointed in the direction of Big Howie. It seemed like a number of clues cried out to be noticed and decreed that it was Howard Simkey who had started the fire at the house in Lakeside. The footprints that were found in the snow at Lakeside were those of a size 13 work shoe with a distinctive tread. It was the same type and size of shoe that Big Howie wore. There were also the empty gas tanks that were found in Howard Simkey's neighborhood, and the smell of gasoline on the bed of his truck. And how about those faint footprints found at the Bedford House? Although they were not as prominent as the ones found at Lakeside, the Duluth detectives noted that they were large—probably size 13 shoes. And where had Big Howie been in the hours before the fire? He said that he'd had too much to drink and that he'd gone home. There were no witnesses to confirm that he'd been at home. Some of the bar crowd said that he'd left the bar after lunch about 3 p.m. The bartender confirmed that. He also said that Howie'd had a lot to drink, and that he hadn't come back to the bar that evening.

So I kept thinking that it was time for me to

talk to Big Howie. Talking to Big Howie was the last thing I wanted to do. I didn't even want to look at him, let alone talk to him. But I had to talk to him, and hear what he had to say. And that would be the hard part, to get him to talk to me. I had to confront Big Howie and get him to tell me something. I needed to hear him say that he'd done it or that he hadn't done it. I could easily see that big shit burning that house to the ground. But I couldn't be sure. I knew he'd done a lot of bad things to a lot of people. He'd beat his ex-wife, and she claimed he'd killed her poodle, but it was never proven. He'd drink, get drunk, and get into bar brawls. He was always bullying or bothering someone. Once he got into a big argument with the manager of his landscaping company because she'd gone out with someone he didn't like. He threatened her and got into a fight with the guy she dated. He also threatened some customers who complained about the workmanship of his remodeling projects. Once, he'd even tried to bother Ellen, and she'd reported him to the Duluth police. That had happened when I was working in Washington, D.C. Mom had told me about it during one of our telephone calls. Even though Ellen had been married back then, when I heard about it, my first thought was to bash Big Howie's head in with a big rock.

Based upon a lot of incriminating evidence, Detective June Brown leaned on Big Howie and asked him a lot of pointed questions. He was their prime suspect. He was even given a lie detector test, but the results were inconclusive.

Big Howie had hated me the first time we met in Duluth, and he probably still hated me now that I was back in Duluth. Although his hatred was strong, I didn't believe it was strong enough to make him kill someone who was innocent and never had done anything to him. I also had a big problem with "LEAVE JEW. DON'T SELL HERE. OR WORSE WILL HAPPEN." What would he care about my selling real estate?

30

Howard Simkey hung out at the Real Duluth Grill, a downtown Duluth bar that served a variety of hamburgers, french fries, other grill food, and plenty of drink and beer. It was the kind of place where you could eat and drink and play pool at the same time. I was told that I could find him there most weekdays after five and sometimes earlier. I wasn't looking forward to talking to him, but I also had some questions that needed answers. I knew that the Duluth detectives were leaning on him—heavily enough to break his back. So I wanted him to know that I had my doubts—serious doubts about his implied involvement. I also wanted to find out if he knew anything, and what he thought about what was going on.

I got to the bar at about 8 p.m. Although it was downtown, it was off the beaten path and kind of seedy looking from the outside. I had felt more comfortable driving the Blazer than the Jaguar. When I pulled into the parking lot, I really felt relieved that I'd gone with the Blazer. It fit in nicely with the pick-ups and other trucks already parked there. I entered the bar. It was smoky, and the yellowish glimmer from far too few light bulbs, combined with the haze from the smoke, made the place look dark and dingy. There was a good size crowd there, probably more than one-half of capacity. I worked myself to the bar and ordered a beer.

I looked around slowly and took in the crowd. Big Howie was at the other end of the bar, drinking, smoking, and yapping at this husky little lady who had a lot of makeup painted on her face. I didn't want to interrupt anything, so I just continued to take in the sights, and tugged at my brew now and then. When the painted lady headed for the restroom, I moved toward Howard Simkey and said, "Howard, I need to talk to you. I'd like to ask you a few questions."

He must have had a good number of drinks in him. He looked at me, his face groggy and a dull glaze over his eyes, then, upon recognition, with angry crazy-looking eyes. He yelled, "You fucking, troublemaking Jew," and ran at me with his arms and hands out in front of him and his head down, like a mad bull seeing red all over.

I moved out of the way just before impact and tripped him, and he hit the bar and fell down. I said, "Look, I don't think you did those things. I just need to ask you some questions."

Cursing and mad as hell, he got up, grabbed a wine bottle, and came at me again. I deflected him by pushing a barstool hard against his knees. As he was startled by the pain of wood against flesh, I moved quickly toward his side and hit him hard in the neck. There was no rock this time, just bare fist and knuckles.

He staggered to the side a bit, and I hit him in the side, then in the stomach, my fist sinking deep into a heap of fat and flesh. As he slumped forward, I put a knee in his face, and he fell backward, holding his jaw and his face in pain. He moved slowly on the ground, hurting and not getting up.

The bartender told me to leave. He didn't want any more trouble. I hesitated for a moment, but it seemed like good advice, so I left. It was about 9:15 p.m. Enough sleuthing for one night.

31

The sooner I power up this Blazer, get out of here, and get home, the happier I'll be. I'm feeling stressed and I'm cold. I'll take a hot shower and get rid of this smoke smell. Then I'll pop some corn, grab a Diet Coke, watch a movie, relax, and unwind. I started the Blazer's engine and felt my hands shaking on the steering wheel. I waited a few minutes. The Blazer warmed up and so did I. I started the drive home.

It should take about forty minutes to get home tonight. Especially tonight. It is dark and cold, and a steady mix of sleet and snow is slowly falling. A better-lit road would have been nice, but there are hardly any cars on the road, so hopefully it won't be too bad. If there's one thing I hate, it's driving in the snow. What I hate even more is driving in the snow in the dark. I'll just take it slow and easy and get home safe and sound. I'll keep the speed at a steady 45 miles an hour. That should do it.

I suddenly see headlights in my rear-view mirror—a car or a truck coming up on me fast. I move from the middle lane to the right lane to let him pass. He moves to the right too. He's still coming up fast. I look in the rear-view mirror again. It's a pick-up truck. Shit, it's Big Howie!

BROKER'S OPEN

This guy doesn't quit. I hit the accelerator and speed up as he bumps the Blazer. I need to do something before he runs me off the road. I can't outrun him; it's too dangerous with the snow on the road. I might lose control and run myself off the road. I can't stop and have him crash into me—I'd be a goner for sure. I'll keep the speed up for now and move to the far left lane. He does the same.

The road turns slightly to the left up ahead. I see the shoulder on the right, a glimpse of some brown grass or dirt, and maybe a small ditch. I turn hard to the right and slam on the brakes. He swerves to the right. My Blazer skids onto the shoulder and into a wide, not too deep ditch. His pick-up truck skids about ten yards past me onto the shoulder and then out of sight.

It feels like the Blazer is rattling all over, but I realize it's me that's shaking. My hip, side, and shoulder hurt from where the seat belt restrained me. I get out and try to run over to where Big Howie's truck went off the road, but my legs feel like lead weights are attached to them. Everything seems to be moving in slow motion. When I finally get there, what I see looks bad. His truck went down a ravine and rolled over. I climb down to try to help him, but he's pinned inside the truck and in bad shape. There are many gashes, and a lot of blood on his face and head. There are broken, jagged pieces of glass everywhere. I smell gas and a burning odor, but there's no smoke or flames. I try to talk to him and get him out of the truck, but he's stuck. He's semi-conscious and mumbling something. I get closer to hear, and I ask him if I can do anything before I go for help. He continues mumbling. I ask him if he killed Sherry Stensgard. He stammers, "You, you, I would kill you. It should have been you."

As I turn to go for help and take a few steps, the truck explodes. I feel the tremor from the explosion and the hot air against the back of my neck from the burning mass of metal. The heat hits my face as I turn to look at the truck, now engulfed in flames. I'm thinking that no one deserves to be burned alive. Not even Howard Simkey.

I climb up the embankment to the road, and go back to the Blazer. Now I feel wet and cold all over. I start up the Blazer and turn up the temperature. I try to get the Blazer out of the ditch. Okay, let's see what this four-wheel drive can do. But the Blazer is lopsided in the ditch, and nothing happens. There's an emergency road kit in the Blazer, and I light some flares on the road. I turn on a flashlight while I'm standing by the road. The snow is still falling. It's a strange sight. All this pure white snow and the bright red flares. And down below, Big Howie in his truck, burning and blackening in the raging fire.

A car approaches and stops. I explain what happened and that I need to get to a phone. We drive about six miles to a telephone, and I call the

Duluth police. I explain what happened again and tell them that they need to send a squad car, fire truck, and an ambulance as soon as possible. I give them additional details and the location of the accident. I tell them it's imperative that they contact Detective June Brown immediately and tell her that there was an automobile accident involving Howard Simkey and Larry Stone.

We drive back to the accident scene. I thank the couple in the car, and they ask if they should hang around. I tell them that it's best if they do and that the police will probably want a brief statement from them.

Detective June Brown arrived ten minutes after the squad car came. By that time, a fire truck and an ambulance were there as well, and the place was beginning to look busy. June hurried over to where I was getting ready to give a statement to the officer in charge. She looked at me and said, "Jeez, Stone, you look terrible." Then to the officer, "What've we got so far?"

He replied, "A burned pick-up truck in the ravine, driver dead. I was just getting ready to take a statement."

Detective Brown asked, "How about those two?"

I said, "They stopped and helped me get to a phone."

She glanced at them and then at the officer. "Okay, officer, get a statement from those folks, so they can be on their way. Also get the coroner out here. Did you call for a wrecker? Take care of that too. And make sure our guys are here to work with the coroner on the dead guy."

Detective Brown turned to me and frowned. She said, "Stone, you come with me."

I followed her to an unmarked car and got in the back. The warmth from the car's heater felt good on my body and began to take the chill out of my bones. I could have closed my eyes and rested, but I knew better.

Detective June Brown looked disturbed and worried. I'd have to say, definitely more disturbed than worried. In an exasperated but authoritative voice, she asked, "Okay, Larry, what the heck happened?"

I began to retell the evening's events. "Well June, earlier in the evening I went to this bar and grill to talk to Howard Simkey. He didn't want to talk and tried to smash me up. He had a number of drinks in him, and while defending myself, I was able to smash him up instead. It was probably quite a show for the bar and grill's customers. I got out of there while he lay groggy on the floor, and I started to drive home. I didn't see anyone following me, and then all of a sudden, he's right on my tail and coming at me fast. He bumps me, and I try to get away. I slam the brakes and skid off the road, crashing into that ditch. He skids off the road and down that ravine. I go over to try to help him. His truck explodes. There were fire and flames all over. His crash was worse than mine."

"Listen, Larry. All this fighting and car crashing." June looked bewildered. She said, "I thought you were a police psychologist. What gives here?"

"You're right, June. I used to be a police psychologist, but I was also a detective in homicide."

"Okay, Larry, let's get this down on paper and then get you to a hospital." June took my hands, and held them in hers for about twenty seconds. Her hands felt nice and warm. "Look at you, Larry! You're wet, chilled, and shaking. We'd better make sure you're okay."

"I'm okay, June. I don't think I need to go to a hospital, but my truck is stuck in the ditch."

June looked at me the way an aggravated mother would look at her son who had just misbehaved. In a no-nonsense voice she said, "Don't worry about your truck. We'll tow it to headquarters and look it over. Come by my office tomorrow morning so that I can get an official statement. I also have some additional questions to ask you and you have some explaining to do."

She turned her head and called out the window, "Officer, please drive Mr. Stone to Duluth General."

Detective June Brown glared at me. I said nothing. She told the officer, "Then make sure he gets home safely."

Her glare softened a bit as she looked back at me and said, "Unless you have some other plans for the evening, Mr. Stone."

I replied, "No, Detective, I don't have any other plans."

"That's good. Is there anything else I need to know at this time, Mr. Stone?"

"No, Detective."

"Okay then. I'll see you tomorrow."

32

I arrived at Police Headquarters about 10 a.m. the next morning for my meeting with Detective Brown. The desk sergeant was expeditious as he escorted me to her office. It seemed as though he was prepped and expecting me. Detective Brown was on the telephone when we entered her office. She beckoned me to sit down. The desk sergeant left. When she completed her call she sat back in a relaxed position and stretched her hands behind her neck. She smiled, a nice warm smile I thought, and she asked me how it had gone at the hospital and how I was feeling. I smiled back and told her that they had checked me over for about fifteen minutes and then sent me home. There were some bruises here and there, but nothing was broken.

Detective June Brown looked tired but relieved. She spoke in a soft but confident voice, "Well, it's finally over, Larry." She went on to explain, "Howard Simkey, Big Howie, committed the murder of Sherry Stensgard at Bedford House. He also started the fire in the other house that resulted in the death of the dog and the total destruction of house and personal property. Then he tried to run you off the road and kill you after your confrontation with him. Fortunately for you, fate stepped in, and Howard Simkey, in an inebriated condition, lost control of his vehicle and toppled down the ravine to his death. The evidence and turn of events point to and support the conclusion. That's what we'll give to the press. That's it. It's over." Just as June finished speaking, a frown began to form across her face. As she stared at me, the frown grew larger and she said, "Oh, no. You have a strange look on your face, Larry. What's the matter?"

I rested my chin on my hand. I slowly turned my head from side to side as I said what I was thinking, "I'm not sure it's over yet, June. I'm not sure it's him."

June looked perplexed. "Not him? What do you mean not him, Larry?"

I continued my train of thought, "It's just a gut feeling I have, June. Things don't add up right. Everything doesn't fit together. The murderer's messages and references to not selling real estate here in Duluth. What did Howard Simkey care about me selling real estate? Also, when his truck went off the road and plunged into the ravine, when I got to him, his face and head were gashed and all bloody. There was broken glass everywhere, and he was pinned under the truck, in very bad shape. I tried to get him out, but I couldn't. Just before the truck caught fire and exploded I asked him if he had killed Sherry Stensgard at the open house. He stammered and said, 'You, you, I would kill you. It should have been you.' "

"Larry, that's almost a confession right there," she said with renewed confidence.

"Maybe, June, but when he said it, it didn't sound like a confession. I would have felt a lot more comfortable if he had said, 'Yes, but it should have been you.' Also, there was that nasty business with the 'For Sale' sign, the way it was plunged into her stomach. That was diabolical, not your typical barroom brawling type stuff, but the work of a real psycho. I'm not convinced it's Big Howie's style, nor is it his profile either." I tried to smile, but the best I could do was tighten my lips a little, as I added, "But I can be wrong. I hope I'm wrong."

"I hope you're wrong also, Larry. In fact, I'm sure you're wrong. Don't forget that he tried to run you off the road—to hurt you or kill you. And a while back we had a complaint from Howard Simkey's ex-wife. She said that he'd killed her dog. She also said that she'd confronted him and that she knew he'd done it, but that she couldn't prove it. There was no evidence. He was questioned but never charged. There have also been complaints that he threatened people, not to mention a number of pushing and punching incidents. And I'm told that in his youth, it was rumored that he pushed a teacher down a flight of stairs. There was no proof, and no charges were filed. I was also told that he was accused of setting the high school on fire. *You* should remember that incident, Larry."

"Yes, June, I do remember that, from my amateur sleuthing days. Thanks for reminding me."

"Don't mention it, Larry. It's my pleasure." June paused. Her face displayed no particular emotion. Then she said, "So, this messy business is finished. This case is officially closed. You've helped us a lot, and I appreciate that. I hope to see you around, Larry."

We both stood up at the same time. June walked over to me and as I put my hand out to shake hands with her, she gave me a hug and said, "Don't be a stranger, okay?"

I'm not sure whether I hugged her back as I said, "Okay, June, I won't."

33

This time I hope I'm wrong. I want to be wrong. The police say it's an open and shut case. Big Howie was the Bedford Murderer. That's it. So why don't I just forget about these thoughts that keep running through my brain, telling me that things just don't add up and that Big Howie is a "no" and not a "yes"?

The problem is that I can't forget about these thoughts. They're too persistent, and I'm unable to make them go away. And this gut feeling that I have—why can't I just let it go? It keeps telling me that the motives don't match the crime and that the information and facts related to the crime are as jagged as the shores of Lake Superior, like defective pieces of a puzzle that won't ever fit together. My gut also tells me that Big Howie is a red herring. And a big red herring at that. I tried to let this gut feeling go, but it keeps gnawing and grinding inside me, and refuses to leave. But why should it leave? My gut feelings have been right in the past.

If not Big Howie, then who? And why lead a path to Big Howie? There were the size 13 shoes, and the matching shoe sole tread, the empty gasoline container found in a garbage can not far from where he lived, and the smell of gasoline in the back of his truck. Who else in Duluth has a size 13 shoe and the same shoe sole tread as Big Howie? Or are all these clues bogus clues? If so, why bogus clues? Who knew that he hated me so much? Why am I a problem now, if I was not a problem then, when I sold real estate back in my college days? I was Jewish then, and I'm still Jewish now. Who knew I was Jewish then? Who knows I'm Jewish now? Maybe Big Howie was the murderer, and I'm making much more of this than I should. But if he wasn't, who knew enough about the two of us back in high school to be able to use that information now?

There are just too many things about this "officially closed case" that bother me. As hard as I try, I can't seem to get the motives, facts, and occurrences to come together in closure. They make me feel that this case is just as open now, if not more open, than it was the day that Sherry Stensgard was brutally murdered. There was something else too. From a police perspective, things went too easily. I remember what Detective June Brown had said, "A disgusting dirty killing done cleanly. We're dusting every inch of the house, but initial reports indicate nothing, no clues, no leads." So how is it that the murder was planned and pulled off so perfectly with no apparent clues? And then the house burning incident was sloppy, and there were a number of clues that were found, all leading to Big Howie. There was also another note sent to me with a message similar to the first, tying both incidents together as the work of the same person.

It was almost like building a path for everyone to follow. It was a road with carefully placed road marks that led the Duluth police and me in the direction of Big Howie and pegged him as the prime suspect. It was a road that I followed, which resulted in a confrontation with Big Howie and his accidental death. However, it could have easily been my death instead, either way would have worked. If it had been my death, then I'd be gone and Big Howie would take the rap for my death and Sherry Stensgard's murder. They would throw in the house burning and death of the dog too. The real murderer gets rid of me and gets away scot-free. With Big Howie's death, the suspected murderer is dead, the case is closed, and the real murderer is still at large, free to plan some other way to get rid of me. The first way is better for him. It's a gamble as to which way it will go, but there is nothing for him to lose. At best, he gets rid of me. At worst, I'm still around but it's the end of the investigation. He could try again. He could try to get rid of me some other way.

I need to look hard at all the information and focus on all the possible motives in this case. I need to develop some linkage and a model, an alternative road to follow, something that will provide a new and better direction. What do I have so far in the way of motives and facts?

Larry Stoller

What's missing here? What am I not seeing?

<u>MOTIVES</u>

Get rid of someone the murderer hates
Get rid of someone the murderer is threatened by
*Get rid of someone who has taken something from
 the murderer*
Make Stone leave Duluth
*Eliminate the Jew, Stone, from selling real estate in
 Duluth*
*Eliminate Stone from selling expensive real estate
 in Duluth*
Eliminate Stone from selling Bedford House
Get the big listings with Stone gone
Make more money with Stone gone
Stop Bedford House from being sold
Get Jews out of Duluth
*Make the real estate business less attractive and
 thin the realtor ranks*
Eliminate realtor competition in Duluth
Get Ellen without Stone around

As I read through these motives, I sense that some are primary and others secondary. I have a stronger sense that the murderer wants to get rid of me because I have taken something from him and he is threatened by me, and for those reasons, he hates me insanely. My being Jewish might make him hate me more. Maybe Bedford House is what started everything in motion, but I'm not sure. Ellen wasn't seeing anyone when I got back to Duluth, when I started seeing her, so I should be safe there.

FACTS

Stone returns to Duluth
Stone starts seeing Ellen Westphal Sommers
Stone becomes instant broker and partner of All Duluth Realty
Stone is in Duluth for eight weeks before murder and fire
Stone lists Bedford House Mansion overlooking Lake Superior—a very prestigious listing
Broker's Open is scheduled
Realtor Sherry Stensgard is murdered at Broker's Open
It is a horrible and brutal murder
She is strangled and hit on the head
A "For Sale" sign is plunged into her stomach
"NOT" written in blood just before the words "For Sale" on the sign
No valuables are taken from Sherry or from Bedford House
Stone receives a note at the office under door, "LEAVE JEW, DON'T SELL HERE, OR WORSE WILL HAPPEN"
Stone gets second big listing
House is burned to ground two days after listing
Stone receives second note with a similar message
Dog in house perishes in flames
All house possessions destroyed except jewelry

and valuables in a safe

No clues found from Sherry Stensgard's murder in mansion

A lot of clues found around house that burned to the ground

Clues lead to Big Howie: gasoline can, gasoline smell, footprints, size 13 shoe, similar shoe sole tread

Big Howie implicated in house burning

Big Howie is investigated by police

Big Howie becomes prime suspect

Big Howie confrontation and fist-fight

Big Howie dies in accidental car crash

Police allege that Big Howie was the Bedford Murderer and that he was responsible for the house burning as well

Gave list of people who hate Stone to Detective Brown

Big Howie hated me and made derogatory remarks about me being Jewish

Rock incident with Big Howie in 1958

Everyone who played in that football game in 1958 knew that Big Howie hated me

Stone attended East HS, 1958 to 1962

Stone made at least one enemy there, maybe more

Report Big Howie to police after very suspicious fire in the chemistry lab at school

Who else back in East HS knew that Big Howie hated me?

BROKER'S OPEN

My aggressive real estate practices when I started
  selling real estate after high school and during
  college
My discount commissions, variable commission
  rates, rebates to buyers
Significant connection to real estate community

Which realtors would have had knowledge of Big Howie and me from high school days? A match of all high school students/graduates from East High School between 1958 and 1962 to current realtors and brokers might reveal that information.

Is there any connection that goes back to high school and/or real estate when I was just helping Ruby? Are any graduates now selling real estate? What about any connection with Ellen—an old boyfriend, a current boyfriend, any current admirers or suitors? Did anyone have a crush on her besides me in high school? I saw Ellen in our last year of high school and all during college. Is there anything from those days that I could remember? What about when I returned to Duluth and started seeing Ellen again, could there be a jealous associate or a patient of hers?

I have to go through both lists and any other information that was available during those dates and times of the murder and house burning. While reviewing the information, I have to keep thinking about the motives and the facts. This someone hates me insanely, to commit such a brutal crime. I'm finding it hard to relate to that degree of hate. What did I do that would make someone hate me that much? He doesn't want me to sell real estate in Duluth. He doesn't want me to even be in Duluth. Why not just kill me? Maybe he wants to, but he wants to hurt me as well. I can't be hurt if I'm dead. I think about the "Jewish angle," but I'm pretty sure that this someone would hate me even if I were not Jewish. He probably hates me more since I am Jewish. I have to read the lists repeatedly. I'll highlight the items that seem more important, and maybe delete some others. Or I'll put the more important ones ahead of the less important ones. I have to stay focused on the motives and the facts. The most significant connection appears to be to real estate. Is that valid or is there something missing? I need to concentrate on real estate, real estate brokers, real estate agents, real estate companies currently active in Duluth. Which real estate companies are doing most of the business? Who are the top producers? Which companies deal with residential versus investment real estate, higher-priced homes versus lower-priced homes, and historic older homes versus contemporary and/or newly built homes? This may not be a valid analysis, as most real estate companies will go after and take any business that comes their way. I also need to determine if there are any ties to All Duluth Realty. Which other companies competed for the Bedford House listing? And are there any ties that go back to my high school days from 1958 to 1962? That's where the investigative emphasis needs to be placed.

I called Danny O'Neill in Washington, D.C. I explained my dilemma to him. I asked him if he would consider spending some time in Duluth and helping me out with this open and shut case. I also told him that I was worried about Ellen and Jane. He immediately said yes, and added that he was looking to get away for a few weeks. I thanked him and told him that I was relieved that he could be here and that I would look forward to seeing him.

Dannyboy will be very helpful in obtaining and analyzing the information that is currently available. Maybe he'll be able to tie in the Duluth police interviews of brokers and realtors to my lists of "motives" and "facts." As a new face in Duluth, he might also be able to obtain additional information from the broker-realtor community.

34

Ellen and I were closer now than we had ever been before. Our song of love was in tune, and we embraced and enjoyed each other physically and emotionally. Our lovemaking was powerful, passionate, and mutually fulfilling. It began tenderly, like gentle ripples in a lake. Then it became powerful, like the riptides during an ocean's storm. It took control of body and mind. It drained our strength and senses. And then it left, leaving us depleted but satisfied. Our acceptance of each other was unconditional, and we were able to open our minds and hearts to each other and share our innermost selves. We were able to give ourselves to each other completely, always knowing that we were safe and secure.

I shared my thoughts about the case with Ellen. At this time, I opened up a Stone box in the back of my brain and let some troublesome thoughts come out.

In a serious and assured voice I said, "Ellen, I don't believe it was Big Howie."

Ellen looked at me in astonishment. As she caught her breath, she said, "What? Not Big Howie! But the police said it was him, and the newspapers. Everyone said it was him."

"That's true, Ellen, but the profile is not right. I spoke with June, and she's certain that this murder case died at the same time that Big Howie died. I discussed psychological profiling with her, and I suggested that Howie's profile did not fit the murder at Bedford House. She listened, and she came back with a number of reasons why Howie's profile was right. And what she said made a lot of sense."

Ellen regained her composure. "But you're not convinced, Larry? You have reasons to believe otherwise," she said slowly and thoughtfully.

I explained, "No, Ellen, I'm sorry to say I'm not. You see, I think that in a drunken rage, Howard Simkey was capable of doing those things in a dumb kind of a way. But I can't see him carefully planning that murder the way it was planned, and then having enough nerve to go through with it, and doing it exactly the way it was done. What was done was diabolical, the work of a real sick mind. Sick but smart. There were no clues to be found. It was planned perfectly. It's definitely not the Big Howie profile. Also, Ellen, why the reference to 'Leave Jew. Don't sell here. Or worse will happen.' It doesn't fit Big Howie either. These disconnects are very disturbing."

"So what happens now, Larry?"

"Well, I'm not sure, but to make matters worse, there are some other things that are bothering me, Ellen."

Larry Stoller

"What other things?"

"Well, in the house-burning there were a number of clues, and they all led to Big Howie— the footprints, the shoe size, the shoe sole tread, the empty gasoline tank, and the gasoline smells from the bed of his truck. There's the similar message to me, but now these clear clues are jumping up and down and into our lap from all over the place. There was nothing before, and a lot now. It doesn't add up, Ellen."

Ellen looked at me. Her eyes were clear and bright and her lips moved slowly, creasing slightly at the ends as she said, "So what's your next move, Detective Stone? I've got a feeling you have a next move, Larry."

"Well, Ellen, I was thinking, maybe it's time to have that broker's open again at Bedford House. If the police are right, and I hope they are, everything should go smoothly. That should reduce my anxiety and hopefully eliminate my fears."

"What fears, Larry?"

"I'm worried about you and Jane. Remember what the note said, 'or worse will happen.' Maybe he'll try to get to me by getting to you." Now Ellen looked frightened. I paused and took her hands in mine. Then, very reassuringly, I said, "Ellen. Do you remember that close friend I told you about, Danny O'Neill, Dannyboy from D.C.? If you happen to see him now and then, although you probably won't, he's up here at my request. I asked him to help me figure out what's going on here, if anything still is, and to watch over you and Jane."

Ellen looked nervous as she said, "I'm scared. But I shouldn't be, right, Larry? This Dannyboy is good at what he does, and besides there may not be any murderer still loose in Duluth, right?"

"Yes, Ellen. Danny's the best. I'm just being very cautious, until I'm certain that this thing is really over. One other thing, Ellen. There's enough real estate business in Duluth for everyone. You wouldn't think my selling real estate, if that was the only thing that was bothering him, would make him go off the way he did. I've got to believe there's more to it." I looked at Ellen for a moment without saying anything. She was so beautiful. And I was so happy that we loved each other the way we did. I finally said what I wanted to say, "Ellen, have there been any admirers or crazed suitors in your past that I should know about?"

"No, Larry. Just you."

"Hmmm. I walked right into that one, didn't I? How about your current practice, Ellen? Does it cater to the Duluth neurotic rich or to the Duluth psychopaths and psychotics as well?"

"The clientele varies, Larry. For the most part, many of my clients have family-and-marriage-related problems. There are one or two individuals who believe that everybody in the world is out to get them. Sometimes, I wonder if I'm helping them at all. There are some others with lesser problems—how to cope with work or how to get along with people better. There is one man who is worried about how he will be remembered after he has gone. He's got a lot of money, and he wants to use it to make a meaningful contribution during his life—do something good that he'll be remembered for. So there's my practice, Larry. What do you think?"

"I think I want to give you a big hug and hold you close to me, Ellen."

"I don't see what that has to do with my practice, Larry, but I love when you hug me and hold me. Anything else on your mind, Larry?"

I put my arms around Ellen and hugged her. I held her close to me and gently kissed her on the lips. She kissed me back and her tongue wet the inside of my mouth. I got very hard. She looked at me and smiled. I smiled back and said, "Yes."

35

The *Duluth News Tribune* had splashed the story all over the front page. "BEDFORD HOUSE ALLEGED MURDERER KILLED IN FIERY CAR CRASH—Police report that Howard Simkey died in an explosive and fiery car crash, hours before he was to be charged for the murder of real estate agent Sherry Stensgard."

The killer's voice was filled with anger and frustration.

"Big Howie, the Bedford Murderer. What a joke! How about Big Fat Stupid Howie, who could not murder a freaking fly. I gave him the opportunity to kill Stone. I got him angry enough to do it, and what does he do? He gets himself killed. The Bedford Buffoon would be more like it!

"So Stone is still around. Everyone believes the Bedford Murderer is dead, and the case is closed. There's no more danger, everyone's safe, Stone included. So now the Jew can stay in Duluth. He can sell prime real estate. He can have Ellen, my Ellen. This goddamn Jew who had no right to even be here in Duluth could now stay and take everything that would belong to me. No. I think not!

"It's time to deal with Stone directly; he needs to disappear forever. No one expects anything to happen now that the Bedford Murderer is gone.

Larry Stoller

But now's the perfect time for something to happen. A fast clean kill and it's all over. Then, I can pursue the big listings with no shitty Stone competition. Only then, I can pursue Ellen as well. My sweet Ellen. It's just a matter of time until she comes around. First it was Stone. That was puppy love. And that ended on its own when Stone left. Sweet Ellen, she wasn't quite ready for my kind of love. Poor Ellen, she needed to be hurt by love a little first. Then it was her husband, but I got rid of him easily enough. And now it's Stone again! It's a simple solution, just kill Stone.

"I have worked too hard to get Ellen. I've worked too hard for the Duluth real estate business to have this Stone come in here and talk about seller discounts, lower commission rates, and buyer rebates. I have waited too long for Ellen to have Stone come here and take her from me. It's time to rid Duluth of this meddlesome Jew.

"No more Bedford Murderer. Realtors all over Duluth can feel safe again. Stone can feel safe again. Let him feel safe. He won't be soon. I'll see to that. I gave him a chance to leave Duluth. But did he? No, he stayed here. Let him sell houses in New York, but not here. Let him find some Jewish bitch, one of his own kind. If Stone won't leave Duluth, then Duluth will leave Stone. Leave Stone dead. I like that, it has a nice ring to it, 'Stone dead.' I'll see to that!"

36

It didn't matter whether this case was officially closed or officially open. For me it was open and it was open more now than it had been before. I thought about my final confrontation with Big Howie. I was the last person to see his face and hear him speak before he died. Although I'd seen and heard both hatred and rage, I had not seen nor had I heard the Bedford Murderer.

Danny O'Neill came to Duluth to help me with this investigation and to keep an eye on Ellen and Jane. I didn't know where the investigation was going or where it would lead or how it would end. I did know that I was worried about Ellen and Jane. Dannyboy could be their hidden angel. I felt very relieved that he was here.

I picked Danny up at the airport, in a gray Cadillac that I had rented for him. We had lunch at a restaurant in Two Harbors, which is outside of Duluth, overlooking Lake Superior. After lunch, I unloaded the officially closed Bedford Murder case on Dannyboy. In extreme and excruciating detail, I explained to Dannyboy why I didn't believe that Big Howie was the murderer. I mentioned that every time I thought about that "For Sale" sign plunged into Sherry Stensgard's stomach, I felt unsettled. And the word "NOT" written in blood, and the "LEAVE JEW. DON'T SELL HERE. OR WORSE WILL HAPPEN." notes. No, I couldn't see Big Howie doing that. I could see him beating people up, bullying people, hurting people, watching people shake and shudder when he antagonized them, and enjoying it all. But I couldn't clearly focus on a picture of Big Howie brutally killing Sherry Stensgard, not to mention writing in blood and that hateful note with its threatening message.

On the other hand, I could clearly focus on a picture of Big Howie, in a drunken rage, trying to run my car off the road with his truck. In fact, after that incident occurred, I saw that picture in my mind many times more than I wanted to. Was he trying to hurt me? Definitely. Was he trying to kill me? Probably. Yes, that picture focused clearly for me, with or without drink in him. But no matter how hard I tried, I still couldn't focus on a picture of Howard Simkey killing Sherry Stensgard in the way that she was killed. The more I tried to visualize that picture, the fuzzier it got. It was like a blurred negative that would not develop. It would not materialize in my brain, nor would it appear before my eyes. It always stopped short and left me with a cringing sensation in the back of my head and neck, of danger and uncertainty. I kept feeling that this murder was still unfinished business and that people's lives were still in danger, mine included. Once again, I expressed my concern for Ellen's and Jane's safety. Danny listened to everything that I had to say and immediately suggested that he have someone from his agency fly up to Duluth. He indicated that that person's only responsibility would be to keep an eye on Ellen and Jane. That, he explained, would allow him to be able to work with me more on the actual investigation. I liked that idea!

Dannyboy and I spent long hours over many days reviewing potential links and suspects based upon my sleuthing before his arrival. Dannyboy completed an intensive review of everyone who attended and graduated from East High School between 1958 and 1962. Their last names were matched against all MLS and non-MLS real estate agents and real estate brokers currently doing business in Duluth in 1983. That match produced four real estate brokers or agents.

Dannyboy met with me, and we reviewed the matching records and the additional information that he had discovered. Of the four last name matches, one realtor had the same last name as one of the four graduates, but he had not attended East High School. One realtor had a daughter who had gone to East High School between 1958 and 1962, and was now a nurse. One broker-owner who had attended East High School now owned and operated what used to be his father's real estate company. One other broker-owner had started his own real estate company.

I looked at the names of these graduates of East High School. The one name that got my attention the most was Sam Salinas, Jr. There was something about that name—something that had happened many years ago. I thought about it and then I remembered. It was a fire—a fire in some house.

It happened when I was in high school. My dad had picked up a new listing. Within a week, the house caught fire and burned to the ground. Rumor had it that somebody thought they had seen Salinas Sr.'s car near the scene of the fire. Sam Salinas, Sr. was the broker-owner of Salinas & Associates. The two men were fierce competitors and they didn't like each other. I told Danny that I remembered Ruby once saying "that he wouldn't put it past that Salinas bastard to do something like that."

Sam Salinas, Sr. had started his company in the 1950's, and father and son had worked together in the business until about five years ago. At that time, Salinas Sr. had retired and moved to Arizona. Salinas Jr. had become the new broker-owner of Salinas & Associates. Over the past five years, the hard-driving Salinas Jr. had aggressively courted the Duluth residential real estate market. The company was very successful and had a good foothold in the higher-priced homes market.

Dannyboy had an idea. He'd contact Sam Salinas, Jr. and pass himself off as new to Duluth and looking for an agent. He was Danny O'Neill, a security consultant from Virginia, relocating to Duluth. He'd have a pre-approval loan letter from his lender, and he would be looking for something in the $175,000—$200,000 price range. Danny would interview a couple of agents, and then decide on one. He'd work with the agent with whom he was most comfortable to get the best deal on a house. Danny would mention that he'd called All Duluth Realty and had been told about cash rebates to buyers. He had never heard of that before. He would say that he'd seen the Salinas & Associates advertisement and called them as well. Dannyboy thought he might mention to Salinas that he had spoken to a Larry Stone at All Duluth Realty to see what kind of reaction there was from him.

I suggested that it might not be a bad idea to also review the notes from the interviews that the Duluth police conducted with the brokers and realtors in the community. Maybe there'd be something there worth pursuing, in addition to the brokers and realtors who had ties to East High School during the time that I attended. For example, "Which brokers and/or realtors competed with All Duluth Realty for the Bedford House listing?" I said that I'd speak to Detective June Brown and ask her if it would be okay for Danny to review all the police interviews and information on the case. If she agreed, he could arrange a visit to Police Headquarters.

Larry Stoller

At first, Detective June Brown was sure that she neither needed nor wanted anyone interfering with this case, especially now that it was closed. But I reminded her that when the case was open, it was she who had convinced me to stay in Duluth and see this thing through. I made it clear that if I stayed, I would be conducting my own informal investigation based upon my past experience and life in Duluth. June told me that was okay and she wouldn't interfere, as long as I didn't get in the way, and as long as I shared whatever information I had with her. I told her that would be fine as long as she shared her information with me. She scoffed a bit and put on her tough-woman detective act. We went round and round a bit, but when she realized how determined I was and how helpful or how unhelpful I could be, she decided to cooperate. But she needed to be apprised of everything that was transpiring, had transpired, or was going to transpire. So now she agreed to cooperate again—with the same conditions in place as before—she was to be kept fully informed. She would allow Danny O'Neill to review the broker-realtor interviews. I told Danny that if anything turned up, she was to be made aware of it.

That very next day, Dannyboy met Detective June Brown at 9:30 a.m. at Police Headquarters. They met in a small file room that had seen better days. On the floor by a battered brown wood table were thirteen boxes filled with paper. Around the table were four uncomfortable-looking beat-up wooden chairs. Yellow light shone down from a few bulbs encased in curved metal grates. The light lost most of its luster as it hit the wooden table, but it seemed to become brighter when it was reflected off the white concrete floors. Except for the fact that the furniture and fixtures were old and ugly, nothing matched. It was an interior decorator's worst nightmare.

"Stone told me your name's Danny O'Neill and that some people call you Danny and others call you Dannyboy. What shall I call you?"

"What shall I call you, Detective?"

"In here, Detective Brown. In the outside world, June is fine."

"Okay, Detective Brown. My friends call me Danny, and my close friends call me Dannyboy."

"Okay, Danny. They're all yours," she said, pointing at the boxes. A hint of a grin appeared on her face as she said, "But I think that Stone is on a wild goose chase. The case has been officially closed. But then Stone has his doubts. What with his psychology, problem profiles, unmatched motives, and his gut feelings, you never know."

Danny smiled and agreed, "You've got that 100 percent right, Detective. With Stone, you never know."

"Let me know if you need anything else, Danny, or if you find something." Detective Brown paused briefly and then said, "You know I like Dannyboy. It has a nice ring to it. See you later."

Danny finished a little more than three hours later, and had to leave promptly for his appointment with Sam Salinas, Jr. at 2:30. He thanked Detective June Brown and told her that he had to run, as he had another appointment. The detective looked at him as he rolled down his shirtsleeves and put his suit jacket back on. She asked him if he had found anything. He said that he believed he had found a few things.

"What things?" she said.

Danny asked if they could discuss it later. He suggested that they might get some food somewhere and he'd fill her in. He asked if there was a good restaurant where they could meet.

Detective Brown scribbled the name of a restaurant on the back of one of her business cards. She said, "They have the best hamburgers in town, incredible variety, and the place is pretty private, as restaurants go. Shall we meet at six, Danny?"

Danny replied, "Six sounds good, Detective. See you then."

Before Danny left, Detective Brown said, "You look like you're in pretty good shape, Danny. Do you work out much?"

Danny was surprised by the direct question. He replied, "Yes, Detective. I've got a regular routine."

37

Sam Salinas's office was downtown Duluth, about six miles from Police Headquarters. Danny had enough time to stop for a quick lunch. A hamburger and fries sounded good to him, but when he thought about dinner and the detective's comments about "the best hamburgers in town," he decided on a Cobb salad instead.

About 2:25 p.m., Danny entered a small but attractive old brick building and found the offices of Salinas & Associates, Duluth Residential Real Estate. An attractive woman looked up from the reception desk, smiled, and said, "Hello. Are you Mr. O'Neill?"

He replied, "That's me, and I have an appointment with Sam Salinas."

"Sam is running about fifteen minutes late," she said. "He is on his way here now. He asked that Maggie Henson, one of our agents, talk with you a bit until he gets here. Would that be okay?"

Danny responded, "Yes, it would."

She got on the phone and said, "Maggie, Mr. O'Neill's here. Okay if I bring him back? Oh. Okay, thanks."

She turned to Danny and explained, "Maggie will be right out. Please have a seat."

Danny wasn't sitting for more than thirty

seconds when a woman appeared and said, "Hello. Mr. O'Neill?"

He looked up and said, "Yes." Danny stared at Maggie and smiled. She returned the stare and smiled back. They looked surprised to see each other as they continued to stare, and then burst out laughing. They both had cropped red hair. Danny finally said, "My name's Danny, what a pair we'd make."

She continued to giggle as Danny followed her into her office, where they sat and talked a bit. She said she'd be glad to answer any questions that he had, until Mr. Salinas returned. Danny explained that he was new in town and looking for a house to buy, and that he wanted to get an excellent realtor to help him find the right home. Maggie said that Sam was one of the best. Danny mentioned that he had also scheduled an interview with someone from All Duluth Realty, and that after meeting with both, he would then choose the agent with whom he felt most comfortable. She lowered her voice and said, "Don't mention All Duluth Realty to Sam. They are our competition, and just a while back, they picked up one of the best listings that Duluth has seen for quite some time. It was the old Bedford House mansion. Sam was beside himself that he didn't get it. He went on for weeks about it." She paused, looked down, and continued, "After what happened there, maybe it's just as well that he didn't get it."

Sam Salinas, Jr. breezed in about 2:45 and joined them in Maggie's office. Actually it turned out to be Salinas's office that they were in. "Mr. O'Neill, I'm Sam Salinas. I'm sorry that I'm running a little late today. Thanks, Maggie. Did you get a chance to tell Mr. O'Neill how wonderful Duluth is?"

"We were just about to get to that. I'll leave you two alone. Nice to have met you, Mr. O'Neill."

Sam Salinas, Jr. stood about five-feet-eight. He probably weighed over two hundred pounds, and his weight was almost evenly distributed from head to foot. Aside from a spare tire that he carried around his middle, he looked like a stocky rectangle dressed up in an expensive light gray suit. He wore a blue shirt with a white unbuttoned collar, and a silk-looking red tie hung loosely from a very thick neck. One would guess that it would be quite a difficult task, if not altogether impossible, to button the collar and tighten the tie around his neck. At the very top of the rectangle was a sea of silver wavy hair that tipped a bit over his forehead. Sam had bluish-gray eyes and a full smile that revealed bright white teeth—which any dentist would be proud of. At the bottom of the rectangle were two shiny black leather loafers that looked like fancy golf shoes, and would have been comfortable strolling about at any of the area's finest country clubs.

Sam Salinas, Jr. didn't waste any time. They shook hands at the same time that Salinas smiled and offered Danny a seat at the table, where he spread out a large multi-colored map of Duluth. "So, what brings you to Duluth, Mr. O'Neill?"

Danny said, "I'm here to increase our company's business. Our work is in industrial security."

"Well, you know, Mr. O'Neill, Duluth was a great city of business and industry. It had its heyday back in the early 1900's. But it's still a great city; it's growing again, and I believe it's ready for a comeback."

Salinas pointed to the map. "Here's Duluth, and there's a number of great homes in the $175,000—$200,000 price range. I believe that's the price range that we talked about on the telephone. And here are some prime Duluth areas you might be interested in."

Salinas was very smooth. Danny was thinking that if he wasn't careful, he might actually wind up buying a house in Duluth from Sam Salinas, Jr.

In a confident voice, with just the right amount of sales savvy, Salinas continued, "Some people prefer a view of the lake, others some acreage and wooded privacy. Yet others want to be close to the downtown area. You know, with the right house you could probably get it all, the lake, the woods, and not too far from downtown. Duluth is rich in stately historic homes, elegant Tudors, classic country style homes, and even a number of contemporary homes built over the past few years." He suggested that Danny might want to think about and decide upon a specific geographic area that was appealing to him. "That's a good starting point," he said. "Then we can begin searching for the best home for you. What do you think? What's your pleasure, Mr. O'Neill?"

Danny explained how he wished to proceed. He told Salinas that he had called two real estate companies, his, and another one, an All Duluth Realty. He also indicated that a Larry Stone at All Duluth Realty had mentioned something about receiving a buyer's cash rebate. Danny stated that he was curious and that he intended to meet with an agent from each company.

At the mention of All Duluth Realty and Larry Stone, Danny noticed that Sam Salinas became annoyed and agitated. He bad-mouthed Larry Stone and said that he didn't have to "Jew down his commission." He then tried to convince Danny that it would be in his best interests to work with him. Danny thought about calling him on his derogatory remark, but decided against it. Instead, Danny firmly restated that he would meet with both agents before deciding with whom to work.

The meeting ended with Salinas saying, "Call me when you have decided and then we'll continue our discussion."

38

annyboy arrived at the Cliff House
Restaurant at about 6:00 p.m. and looked
around for Detective June Brown. He
settled in at the bar and ordered a drink. He was
in the mood for a Michelob Light. The cold drink
felt good, and it was nice to relax after a long,
tiring day at Police Headquarters and then going
round and round with Salinas. He kept thinking
to himself, maybe Stone was all wet, and this
whole thing ended when Big Howie died. On the
other hand, Stone sometimes had this kind of
sixth sense, where he was able to think and see
things differently. That way of thinking and
seeing, combined with his gut feelings, enabled
Stone to solve a number of almost impossible
cases back in Washington, D.C. As far as that
Salinas character was concerned, he sure got
upset at the mention of All Duluth Realty and
Larry Stone. He looked like he could go from hot
to cold and then back again at the drop of a hat.
At first he's warm and reassuring. If things don't
go his way, he becomes cool and aloof. It looked
like he could wear whatever face fit the occasion,
change faces if required, and do whatever it takes
to get the job done. He could be dangerous

June joined Danny at the bar. She moved so

quickly and quietly that he was somewhat surprised. She smiled as she said, "Lost in deep thought, Danny?"

"Oh, hello, Detective, I mean June."

"That's better, Danny. How about we get away from the bar and grab a table over there."

"That sounds good, June. Lead the way." He followed June to a corner table. She was a very shapely and attractive woman who looked good from all sides. They ordered, and she asked him what he had discovered. Danny discussed the lists that he and Stone had compiled and that he had compared against police interviews with Duluth brokers and realtors. He said that a few matches had come up, and that this Sam Salinas, Jr. rubbed him the wrong way.

"What do you mean, rubbed you the wrong way, Danny?"

"That was my two-thirty meeting today, June, with Sam Salinas, Jr. I've been thinking about maybe buying a house here in Duluth."

June looked at Danny. She appeared amused or annoyed, or a little of both. She frowned a little and said, "Oh, really?"

"Well, not really, but that's what I told Salinas. I also told him I'd be interviewing a couple of agents, to find the best one to represent me. He and someone from All Duluth Realty, what was his name, ah, a Mr. Stone. I said that Mr. Stone mentioned something about maybe getting a cash rebate if I purchased through him. I'll tell you, June, Salinas wasn't happy. The bigoted bastard said that he didn't have to 'Jew down his commission.' Also, one of his agents mentioned that Salinas was pretty pissed after All Duluth Realty got that big mansion listing."

"You've been busy, Danny."

"A little, but there's something else, June. Stone remembers his dad, Ruby, talking about an incident in which one of his listings caught fire and burned to the ground many years ago. And someone thought they saw Salinas Sr.'s car in the general vicinity at the time of the fire. That's as far as it went. While there were never any other incidents to talk about, neither man liked the other."

"Well, what do you think, Danny?"

"I think Sam Salinas, Jr. is an ass, and probably a real scumbag, but he's got a successful business. He's busy and doing very well. He has employees who seem happy and seem to like him."

"Does he hate Stone, Danny?"

"He probably does." Danny smiled and added, "Probably more so now that we've spoken."

"Enough to kill someone?"

"I don't think so, June. Unless it's Stone."

June half-smiled, shook her head, and said, "Poor Stone. Like he needs someone else to hate him."

Danny slowly nodded his head in agreement, as they stared at each other in silence.

June broke the silence. "Did you find out anything else?"

Danny replied, "I found out who competed with All Duluth Realty for the Bedford House listing. There were three others, a William Preston, a Rose Peterson, and our friend Sam Salinas, Jr.

"According to the information that your guys compiled, Salinas stated that he'd gone to the broker's open at Bedford House, but that he'd been turned away by the police. A number of other agents had the same story. Rose Peterson indicated that she had intended to go to the broker's open, but that she changed her mind at the last minute and did not go. She went shopping instead. William Preston stated that he was vacationing in South Carolina on Hilton Head Island. Your guys were pretty thorough, and they had records of where these brokers and realtors lived, where they worked, and where they went to school. Sam Salinas, Jr. and Rose Peterson attended East High School at the same time that Stone did. William Preston attended East High School also. He was one year ahead of Stone. Stone, Salinas, and Peterson were about the same age. Preston was a year older. I asked my company to run a credit check on the three of them, and to find out about their finances as well. When they get that information back to me, I'll review it and see if there's anything of interest. That's all that I have for now, June."

Danny finished his burger while June was still working on hers. Danny had ordered the "Italian Burger," a half-pound of lean sirloin covered with savory tomato sauce and slices of provolone cheese. It didn't stay around long at all. June looked at Danny's empty plate and said, "What did you think of that hamburger, Danny?"

"One of the best I've had, June. You know your restaurants and you have good taste!"

She smiled and said, "Thanks. I'm glad you enjoyed it. By the way, what do you think about this case, Danny?"

Without hesitation, Danny replied, "Closed and I hope it stays closed, June."

"So do I, Danny. So do I. Listen, Danny. I'm going to catch a movie later. I need to enjoy myself a bit, relax, and unwind." June paused for a moment. "Would you like to join me?"

"Which movie, June?"

"*Sudden Impact*, with Dirty Harry. I mean Clint Eastwood."

"That sounds good to me. What time?"

"It starts at eight-thirty."

"Can I pick you up at your place, June? I want to stop back at the hotel, wash up, and get into some jeans."

"Here's my address, Danny. If you can get there by eight-fifteen, we'll have enough time to get to the movie."

"See you then, June."

At the movie theatre, Danny took off the

parka he was wearing over a classy Snoopy tee shirt. As they sat down, June clasped his heavily muscled arm and said, "Wow, you do work out."

They settled in and watched the movie. They enjoyed watching Dirty Harry do his thing. They were two police people watching a movie about police. They relaxed, unwound, and let Dirty Harry do the police work for a change.

After the movie Danny took June home. It was late, and he thanked her for the invite. At her door, he told her that he had enjoyed seeing the movie and being with her. He said goodnight. She said, "I hope so," and very slowly slid against him and kissed him hard on the mouth—then again, softer and in the french. They were hot. Very aroused, he lifted her off her feet as they continued to kiss, and gently carried her from outside her door to inside her living room. On her living room floor, which was richly carpeted and heavily padded, they satisfied some very hungry appetites. With June clinging to him, and Danny still inside her, he lifted her and carried her into the bedroom, gently pulsating inside her with each step he took. In her bedroom, hot love turned to tender love, and then back to hot again. As the night faded, their loving got stronger, and they held on to the night's magic until morning.

39

Dannyboy and I met the next morning. We had bagels, cream cheese, and lox before getting down to business.

I anxiously asked, "Danny, how'd you make out with Detective June Brown and broker Sam Salinas?"

Danny's response was, "Bad, good, and very good."

Sometimes with Danny, you just have to listen and things become clear. I was thinking in terms of two questions and two answers. What I heard were three answers.

Danny went on to explain, "I spent a good number of hours going through all of the police interviews with Duluth realtors and brokers. The broker who found Sherry Stensgard called the police immediately. They got there before anyone else came and sealed off the entire house. As other realtors showed up, the police took their names and turned them away.

"I wasn't able to come up with much from the police interviews and notes. It didn't look like they had a list of suspects. I didn't find anything from the police interviews that jumped out at me screaming 'madman murderer,' but I did find some information that may be of value to us. I found out which brokers and realtors stated that they visited or attempted to visit your broker's open at Bedford House. That was one of the questions the police asked. The immediate follow-up question was, 'What happened when you got there?' I made a list of the brokers/realtors who stated that they had gone to the Bedford House broker's open that day. There were thirteen in total. Sam Salinas, Jr. was one of them. Why would he want to go to a broker's open that he competed for but didn't get?"

"You said he competed for it?"

"That's right. I obtained the names of those brokers and realtors who competed for the Bedford House listing. That was another question that the police asked during the interviews. It looks like three others competed with All Duluth Realty for Bedford House. They were William Preston, Rose Peterson, and Sam Salinas, Jr. According to the police notes and interviews, Peterson decided not to go to the broker's open. It was a last minute decision. She decided to go shopping instead. Preston was on vacation in Hilton Head, South Carolina, during the week of the broker's open."

I blurted out, "Hilton Head is a great vacation spot, Danny. Preston has good taste." Then, realizing that I had interrupted, I apologized.

Danny smiled and said, "That's okay, Stone. Maybe we should zip down to Hilton Head for a week after this thing is over." He continued, "Let's see, I mentioned Peterson and Preston. Salinas stated that he went to the Bedford open but that he was turned away by the police. All three attended East High School. You, Salinas, and Peterson are about the same age and were in the same grade in high school. Preston was a year older than you and one grade ahead of you. Peterson didn't show up on our initial match of brokers to high school names because she was married. Her husband died a few years ago, and she kept his name. I called one of my guys in D.C. and gave him the three names and their Social Security numbers. I told him to get me a credit report on each of the three and financial information as well. You know how easy it is to get that information—savings accounts, checking accounts, investments, etc. I should have it all by tomorrow.

"I also asked June if she could tell me a little about the personal lives of Salinas, Preston, and Peterson. She said she would get me some information. June wanted to grill me on what I had found and what information I had, but I told her I needed to hustle to get to a two-thirty appointment."

"June?"

"Detective June Brown."

"Ah, Detective Brown. I see."

"Anyway, she was persistent, so we decided to meet for dinner later to go over what I found and what I knew."

I looked at Danny and smiled, "You and June for dinner."

"Jeez, Stone, look at you. You've got this quirky grin on your face. That 'what-else-do-you-want-to-tell-me Stone smile.' You want me to tell you that we went to her apartment and screwed each other the whole night through?"

"Did you?"

"No, we went to see a movie first."

Danny and I looked at each other for a few moments without speaking. A sliver of a smile appeared on Danny's face. "What, Stone? What is it?"

"Oh, nothing," I replied nonchalantly. "I was just thinking. It's good that you and June got along well together. I was also wondering about how your meeting went with Salinas."

"My meeting with Salinas. That was some meeting. You'd get along well with Salinas, Stone. The two of you could play mind games with each other. When we first met, he had a way of engaging me with his eyes and smile, and made me think, 'Here's an honest agent who knows his stuff and would be good to work with.' His voice is very smooth and reassuring. He's top salesman material, this Sam Salinas, Jr. Then, when I mentioned that I planned to interview a couple of agents to find the best one to work with and I started talking about All Duluth Realty and this Larry Stone, I could see quite a change come over Mr. Sam Salinas, Jr. Like it's a sunny day, and then the clouds roll in front of the sun so quickly and quietly that what was light and warm a few seconds ago is now dark and cold. Now his smile seemed to fade. It seemed forced, and his eyes appeared less sincere and helpful. I could sense hurt, frustration, and anger that I would even think about interviewing another agent, especially Larry Stone. I could see that he was upset, and his voice was not as smooth as it had been before. Although he tried to appear understanding and reassuring, with my best interests at heart, I was pretty sure what was going on inside his head. If he had an opportunity to push the 'no more Stone button' and/or the 'no more All Duluth Realty button,' he would hit the Stone button without any additional thought, regret, or remorse whatsoever, and Stone would be gone. All Duluth Realty without Stone might be spared, but I couldn't guarantee it.

"Were there any bad feelings between you and Salinas, Stone? Did you ever mix it up with him in high school or in college?" Danny asked quizzically.

"No, Danny, except he played football with us once, and he was from Howard Simkey's neighborhood and played on their side."

"Is there anything at all, Stone, that you can remember about him?"

"Let me think, Danny. Yeah, Sam Salinas, Jr.—that shithead hung around with Big Howie. He even egged him on to beat me up."

I continued, "Then there was that incident with my dad's listing that I told you about—when that house caught fire and burned to the ground. Even though he had no proof, Ruby always believed that Sam Salinas, Sr. had something to do with it."

"What do you think, Stone? Like father, like son?"

"It could be 'Like father, like son,' Danny. Or how about just 'Like son,' and leave it at that."

Danny continued, "Sam Salinas, Sr. had founded his real estate company two years before Ruby Johnson started All Duluth Realty. Salinas Sr. retired a few years ago and moved to Arizona, leaving the company to Sam Jr. The company was of medium size, fairly successful over the past years, and now more successful under the hard-driving Sam Jr. Sam Salinas, Jr. is smooth, the ultimate salesman. But I managed to ruffle his feathers a little. I told him I was from Virginia and relocating to Duluth, that my work was in the security consulting business, and I was in the process of obtaining some substantial business in Duluth. I even had a pre-approval letter with me for $200,000. Sam Jr. gave me a superb summary of the real estate market in Duluth and asked how much I was thinking about spending. I told him somewhere in the $175,000—$200,000 range. I could have sworn that I saw his eyes light up a bit. He said, 'You could get an exceptional house in that price range. There are a number of them around that are really good deals. It's just a matter of which part of Duluth you'd like to live in. Here's a map. Here's where we are. The lake's here and here are some exceptional homes with great views of the lake.' I pretended to be impressed and interested, but I also told him that I had called two companies, his and another. I added that a Larry Stone at All Duluth Realty said that I could get a homebuyer's rebate through his company. I told him I was curious about that and wanted to meet with agents from both companies before deciding with whom to work.

"Sam Salinas, Jr. was visibly annoyed. It's always amazing how quickly some people can turn the charm on and then turn the charm off. Salinas was definitely one of those people. With a forced smile on his face, but annoyance and anger in his voice, he explained that some agents might offer a nominal cash rebate but come up short on customer service. Whereas he took his job very seriously and professionally, some others, Larry Stone included, relied more on cash-back offers to make up for the lack of service provided. He further explained and guaranteed that with him, not only would I find exactly what I was looking for, but that he would negotiate the lowest price, which would be a much greater savings than a cash rebate. Now get this, Stone; he then says he doesn't have to 'Jew down his commission.' He explains that with his knowledge of the market and negotiating skills, he'll show me how to get the best deal and pay thousands less than the asking price. Then he says, 'So shall we continue with me as your realtor and exclusive representative? I guarantee you'll get the house you want and pay much less. You won't be disappointed.' "

Danny continued, "Stone, this Salinas is so smooth and persuasive. But he's also a bigoted son of a bitch. I got the impression that the phrase 'Jew down' was easy for him to say. It's something he's probably said a number of times before.

"So then I say to him, 'You may become my exclusive representative, but first I will meet with both agents, as I said I would. Then I'll decide.' At that, he says, 'By all means. It's your choice. Call me when you decide, and then we'll continue our discussion.' As I leave, I'm thinking to myself, this guy really hates you. Even if he didn't before, he does now."

"Thanks. That's just what I need, someone else in Duluth who hates me. What do you think, Danny? Does he hate me enough to do the things that someone who hates me already did?"

"Well, I don't know, Stone, but here's the best part. I get there exactly on time and the receptionist says he's running late and will be back in about fifteen minutes. And that Mr. Salinas asked if it would be okay if I spoke with another agent until he returned, a Maggie what's-her-name. So I'm kibitzing with this Maggie, and we're talking about how beautiful the lake is, and this and that, and I mention that I also have an appointment with All Duluth Realty. She giggles and says, 'Well, don't mention that to Sam. Was he ever upset about that mansion overlooking the lake. He was fuming for some time about not getting that listing.'"

40

After Danny had finished telling me about his meeting with Sam Salinas, Jr., he indicated that he would be meeting with William Preston that afternoon and then with Rose Peterson the next morning. They would be the same kind of meeting that he had had previously with Sam Salinas, Jr. He would say that he was relocating to Duluth and looking for a house to buy, and that he needed a good broker or realtor to work for him.

Danny also told me that he should have the credit reports and financial information for Salinas, Peterson, and Preston by the end of the day or next morning at the latest. He then smiled and said that Detective June Brown had promised to obtain personal information and local gossip about the three of them as well.

I asked him why he hadn't set up the meetings for Peterson and Preston on the same day. He indicated that only Preston's name had come up during the high school matches, so he'd set up that meeting right away. He explained that Rose Peterson had also competed for the Bedford House listing, and that the police information revealed that Peterson was her married name. Rose Peterson had attended East High School, but she'd been Rose Salazar before she was Rose Peterson. As soon as he found that out, he had scheduled a meeting with her.

Danny had some time before his meeting with William Preston. He had current color photos of Salinas, Peterson, and Preston, which he shared with me. Those faces looked familiar. I had copies of the East High School yearbooks from 1960 to 1964. I pointed to the books, and said, "Let's see what they looked like back in high school."

Danny eyed the yearbooks and picked one up. He flipped through the pages until he found what he was looking for. His eyes narrowed as he put his finger on one of the photos and said, "Here's a dangerous-looking character, Stone."

As I looked at the photo, Danny burst out laughing. It was a picture of me. I bragged and said, "Yes, dangerous, debonair, and downright handsome as well." We both had a good laugh.

We located a picture of Sam Salinas, Jr. He had a thick short neck, a head of bushy, light-colored hair, and a million-dollar smile. Danny said that Salinas must have practiced a lot to perfect that smile. In the same book, we also found a picture of Rose Salazar Peterson. Rose was very attractive, and she stood out from the other girls. She had long black hair and a beautiful face with prominent features. It was the kind of face that made a guy look twice, and then continue staring. She looked like an Egyptian queen.

BROKER'S OPEN

I continued to flip through the pages while Danny picked up another yearbook. He quickly located a picture of William Preston. Danny indicated that Preston had graduated from East High School a year before Salinas, Peterson, and me. Preston had dark eyes and dark eyebrows on a long thin face, and straight dark hair that was neatly cut and perfectly combed—neat and tidy, and not a hair out of place.

Danny noticed that I was staring intently at an open yearbook. I was holding the book carefully and my eyes were glued to a particular page. I must have had a strange or worried expression on my face, because with some concern, Danny asked me what I was looking at. I slowly pointed to the photo that had caught my eye and would not let go. It was a picture of the girls' tennis team. There was Ellen, looking straight ahead and smiling. Next to her was Rose, with her arm around Ellen, and looking at Ellen. Something about the way that she was looking at Ellen bothered me. I studied the photo very carefully. I moved it closer to my face so that I could see it better. I continued looking, thinking that the picture might tell me something. Danny snapped me out of it. He tapped my shoulder and said, "Hey, Stone. Don't read anything into it. It's just a photo. An old high school photo. Okay?"

I paused and looked away before responding. Then I looked at the photo again, and in a robotic reply I said, "Yes. Just an old photo. Okay." But it wasn't okay. I couldn't stop thinking that Rose was looking at Ellen in the same way that I used to look at Ellen. It was a look of love. With Rose, maybe lust also. And it bothered me.

Tired and feeling disgusted, I said, "Look, Danny, I'm going to drive around Duluth a bit and then walk around a little. I need to clear my head, and then do some more thinking about this 'closed case.' Can we plan to get together tomorrow, after your meeting with Rose Peterson? Call me when you're done, and we'll grab some lunch together. Hey, Danny, thanks for taking the time off to help me with this one!"

41

Danny and I met for lunch the next day. We settled into a private booth in the corner of the Cliff House restaurant. Danny said that he had eaten here once before, and that they had the best hamburgers in town. That sounded good to me. We sat down and ordered and then Danny told me about his meetings. Danny mentioned that he had met with William Preston the previous afternoon and then with Rose Peterson that morning. He also indicated that he had received the financial information and credit reports on Salinas, Peterson, and Preston, and that Detective Brown had provided him with some local gossip as well.

Danny filled me in on Sam Salinas, Jr. first. He said, "Salinas Jr. is about the same age as you, Stone. He took over his dad's real estate company when his dad retired and left Duluth. Salinas is doing pretty well. He hustles hard for the business, makes big bucks, and spends big bucks. He's divorced and has two daughters who live with his wife. His wife has full custody. She has remarried and Salinas has nothing to do with her or the kids. When they split, she complained that he had emptied a couple of joint bank accounts and that he had taken some expensive jewelry from her. She didn't push it, and nothing came of it. It appears that she's pretty well off and that she didn't need, nor did she want, anything from him. She just wanted to get rid of him."

Danny continued, "Salinas drives a fancy black Lincoln, and he enjoys his toys. He has a sports car, a sailboat, and he also owns a condo in Florida on Sanibel Island. Financially speaking, his assets total over five hundred thousand, and he owes on most of what he owns. He's a member of the Duluth Country Club and he likes to mix with the country club crowd, although he's not in their league. He has to keep selling and make money in order to keep mixing. Most of them don't. June mentioned that he was once stopped for drunken driving, but that he talked his way out of it. She also said that during his divorce, the police were called to the Salinas residence a couple of times. Salinas's wife called the police and complained that Salinas was drunk, belligerent, and threatening to her and her two daughters. June also remembers an attorney telling her that Salinas put on such a show that his wife was relieved just to pay him off and be rid of him. He pays no alimony and no child support. It was not your typical divorce settlement. The attorney also told June that he believed that Salinas's behavior was all part of a plan. It was a plan to profit from the divorce and walk away in better financial condition after the divorce than before."

Danny reflected on what he had told me so far and then added, "I'll tell you, Stone. When I first met the guy, he came off so smooth and suave. He was almost charming. Then when things weren't going his way, he did a complete one-eighty. He was able to turn on the charm and then turn it off, like turning a light on or off. But he was easy to get to. When I told him that I was going to talk to another agent, he was visibly annoyed and brought down a notch or two. And when I mentioned that the other agent's name was 'Larry Stone,' he became angry."

"I remember you mentioning that, Danny. I also remember what you said about Salinas being angry enough to push the 'no more Stone button.' I wonder if he'd push the 'no more Sherry Stensgard button.'"

"It's difficult to say, Stone, but as far as Salinas is concerned, I think that he thinks that everyone is expendable, as long as he gets what he wants."

I thought about what Danny had said before replying. "You know, Danny, I never liked the word 'expendable.' It always reminded me of the Service. In the Service, everyone was said to be expendable. When I heard you say 'expendable,' my first thought was, 'I still don't like that word.' However, when I think in terms of Salinas as being expendable, it doesn't sound too bad to me at all."

I then frowned and added, "I don't know what

to do about this Salinas, but I'll think of something. How about William Preston? How did your meeting go with him?"

Danny relaxed a bit and took a drink before continuing. He went on, "I got to Preston's office about one-fifteen for a one-thirty appointment. The receptionist let him know that I was there, and he came out right away to meet me. William Preston—Prestigious Properties was located in downtown Duluth in an old Victorian house. The outside of the house was very attractive and well preserved. It looked better and certainly more inviting than some newer houses that I've seen. The inside of the house was spotless and well appointed with comfortable furniture and quality furnishings. I went through the same routine with Preston that I did with Salinas. I told him that I would be relocating to Duluth and that I would be looking for something in the $200,000 price range or less. Preston gave me a brief but colorful account of Duluth history, and he showed me pictures of Duluth in the early 1920's. He stated that although the current economy of Duluth was not nearly as robust and busy as it had been back then, the city had some exciting plans and economic expansion projects. He also said that this was an excellent time to buy real estate while it was still very reasonable and affordable.

"I listened to what he had to say during the history lesson and afterwards. He was pretty low key but extremely knowledgeable. When he spoke about Duluth and Duluth real estate, he spoke with an air of confidence and conviction. I got the impression that he was talking about 'his Duluth.' "

"What do you mean by 'his Duluth,' Danny?"

Danny explained, "It's difficult to say, Stone, but it's like he's talking about Duluth and Duluth real estate as though it all belonged to him."

"Is he cocky, Danny? Does he have an attitude?" I asked curiously.

"No, Stone, it's not like that. He's just very confident and comfortable. So much so that I get the feeling that he believes that he is the major player and the final authority when it comes to the business of selling expensive Duluth real estate.

"Preston's a year older than you, Stone, and he was one year ahead of you in high school. His father was a real estate attorney who assisted his son, William, in establishing a real estate brokerage. After William Preston completed college, he started William Preston—Prestigious Properties. His dad fed him a number of clients, both big and small, with a silver spoon on a silver platter. Young Preston ate whatever Dad put on the plate. After his dad passed away, Preston inherited the family estate. He's worth about five million now. He only sells what he wants to sell, referring the rest of the business to his agents. He likes selling the expensive properties and therefore limits his dealings to the expensive homes. He has five agents in his company, one of whom is a broker-manager. His name is John Stemmons. If any business comes in that Preston does not want to handle himself, he refers it to John Stemmons. John Stemmons either handles it or refers the clients to one of the other agents.

"After listening to what Preston had to say, Stone, I told him that I had an appointment with another company and that I would decide which realtor I felt most comfortable with, and then choose that realtor to work with. Preston smiled and said that that was the smart way to do it, and that if he were in my shoes he would probably do the same. I said that I would be meeting with someone from All Duluth Realty, what was his name, a Larry Stone, that was it. For an instant, Preston's expression changed and I noticed a flicker of surprise in his eyes. Preston paused briefly, and then he smiled again. It appeared to be less of a smile than before. He picked up his phone and asked someone to come in. Preston introduced me to John Stemmons. He then told John that I was new to Duluth and in the process of choosing a real estate agent to work with in finding and buying a home. He further indicated that he would be unavailable a few days this week and that some of his business interests required him to be out of town next week as well. He stated that he wanted to be sure that they were available for me and that if it was okay with me, he would refer me to John Stemmons. Preston stood up and thanked me for coming into the office. He shook hands with me and said that he hoped that they could assist me, and that John would be available to take care of me.

"John and I went back to his office, and we conversed for a half-hour more before I left. John Stemmons looked to be in his late sixties. He was of medium height and build, and he looked fit for a man his age. He had wavy silver grayish hair and a warm smile. His manner of speaking was eloquent and listening to him suggested that he was happy and comfortable with his work and position in life. John indicated that he used to be in the mortgage business and that he had worked with William Preston's father many years ago. He added that now, and for the past ten years or so, he has managed the Preston brokerage and has sold a variety of houses throughout Duluth.

"I reaffirmed my interest in buying a home and mentioned that I was impressed with Preston and his knowledge of Duluth real estate. John agreed with me and said that Preston's forte was expensive residential real estate. John also said that Preston has a variety of real estate investments that keep him busy as well. So he refers a lot of business to his agents. John Stemmons smiled and said that Preston's a top producer, but that he didn't have to depend on real estate sales to support his comfortable standard of living. I mentioned to John that, speaking of expensive real estate, I couldn't help but notice all the newspaper buzz about Bedford House and the Bedford Murderer. John looked at me and shook his head. He said that what had happened at Bedford House was terrible and that he was relieved and thankful that it was all over now. I told him that I thought Bedford House would be the kind of property that Preston would sell. John agreed that they thought that Prestigious Properties had a good shot at listing Bedford House. But All Duluth Realty had snatched it up. He also said that he was pretty sure that Mr. Preston was upset about not getting it, but that he hadn't made a big deal about it.

"I asked Stemmons why he thought Preston was upset. He replied that Mr. Preston had competed for that listing, and he believed that Mr. Preston was of the mind that Prestigious Properties should get the big listings. John also mentioned that when William Preston started the brokerage, his dad, who was a well-known real estate attorney, steered many clients to his son William. John said that Barrett Preston was a wealthy Duluthian who measured people by how much money they had, where they lived, what they looked like, and what category of Duluth's social system they fell into."

"So, Danny, the social system, though hidden from plain view, is alive and well in Duluth?"

"According to Stemmons, Stone, it was alive and well inside Barrett Preston. And Barrett Preston instilled it inside young William. The

Prestons were and would continue to be part of Duluth's privileged upper class."

"Well, Danny, what do you think? What does William Preston look like? Does he look like Duluth's privileged upper class?"

Danny replied, "William Preston was about five feet nine inches tall. His hair was thin and darkish brown. It was carefully combed and it appeared that every strand of hair knew its proper place. Preston was thin and slight of frame and had a fine tan. It almost looked like it was painted on his face. It was the kind of tan that you didn't get from staying in Duluth all year. His clothing was expensive, tastefully matched, and perfectly tailored. His gold watch and gold ring looked very comfortable on his wrist and finger, almost like they were part of him. He's worth about four or five million, maybe more. He drives a top-of-the-line new Mercedes and most of the things he owns, he owns free and clear. Does he look like Duluth's privileged upper class? Yes, I'd say he does, and I'm sure he thinks he is."

"Okay, Danny, we've got Preston and Salinas in the game now. How about Rose Peterson? Are you saving the best for last?"

"I don't know, Stone. In the business of selling expensive real estate, I don't think that Rose Peterson is in the same league as Salinas and Preston, although I understand that she picks up a big listing every now and then. I met with her this morning at nine-thirty. She started her own company about ten years ago. She has a small office downtown, and she works solo. There's no other agents, no secretary, just her. She seems to be doing well, but she doesn't look like a big hitter and top producer. I'll tell you, Stone, she's some good looker."

With my best Stone smile, I asked, "Yes, Danny, tell me, how does she look?"

"Well let's see, what's the best way to describe her? She's tall and sinewy. She has a strong handshake, and I couldn't help noticing some flexing of the muscles in her biceps."

I was still smiling as Danny continued.

"She stands about six feet tall, very shapely, and her body, arms, and legs are trim and hard. She has short black hair and her facial features are striking, as though they were etched over a layer of tightly drawn olive-colored skin."

"That's pretty good, Danny. You're getting to be quite the man of words. Does she still look like an Egyptian queen?"

"No, not an Egyptian queen, Stone. She's too tall and her hair is too short. There's also some hardness in her face, around her eyes and mouth. No, she looks more like an attractive woman athlete."

"What did she have to say to you after you gave her your spiel, Danny?"

"It was very interesting, Stone. She was very attentive, and she listened carefully to what I had to say. When I was finished, she said that she usually recommends that prospective clients shop around a bit and talk to a couple of different agents. She said that then they would be in a good position to choose the realtor that they felt most comfortable with. She also said that she was sure that she could locate a very nice home for me, and she asked me if I had a loan officer. I told her that I did, and I produced my approval letter. She said that she was impressed and that I was way ahead of the game. She pointed out that most buyers don't think that far ahead. She then asked me if I would tell her a little about the kind of home that I would like. I gave her some of my requirements, and I also said that I would like to be relatively close to both indoor and outdoor tennis courts. In fact, I told her it might be nice to have a tennis court in my back yard, or at least have a big enough back yard to build one. She asked me if I played a lot, and I said that I did. She smiled and said that she played a lot back in high school, and that she now played two or three times a week."

I glanced at Danny and nodded, "That was a good idea, Danny, bringing tennis into it. What else did she say?"

Danny continued, "Well, I said that I didn't think tennis was a big sport in Duluth. I asked her if she was on a tennis team in high school. She said that she was. I asked her if her team won any championships. She said that they won some and that she had great memories of her high school tennis and of her close friends from the tennis team."

"Did she say anything else, Danny?"

"Yes, Stone, we're getting to the good part. I told her that I was scheduled to meet with one other realtor and that then I would decide with whom to work. I told Rose Peterson that I would be meeting with a Larry Stone from All Duluth Realty. She looked directly at me, and it appeared that the skin on her face tightened. I didn't think that her skin could get any tighter than it was. She thought for a moment or two and then said that she knew Larry Stone. She pointed out that Larry Stone was not a native Duluthian, and that he had just recently returned to Duluth after being away for ten years. She also mentioned that he had lived in New York for many years before coming to Duluth, and that he had also lived in Washington, D.C. after he left Duluth. She said that she would be concerned, in that Mr. Stone might not be aware of recent real estate activity in Duluth. Further, she said that he might not know the real value of Duluth real estate, what homes are currently available, and what homes are about to become available as well. I have to tell you, Stone. She looked surprised when I mentioned your name. I didn't read any anger in her voice or her expression, but she definitely knew a lot about you. Probably much more than you knew about her."

Danny continued, "In addition to being

attractive and shapely, she's in pretty good shape financially as well. She was married, but her husband died a few years ago. She kept his name and his money. She has over two hundred thousand split between cash and mutual funds. Her house is free and clear, and she has no appreciable debt. She makes a good income, and her business is doing well. June brought me up to speed on the Rose Peterson local scuttlebutt. Rose has never been in any trouble with the police. There are no complaints on file or pending against her. June mentioned that her neighbors say she's pretty quiet and keeps to herself. Before her husband died, the neighbors said the two of them used to bike a lot and play a lot of tennis. Her husband was diagnosed with bone cancer, and he went from healthy to sick pretty fast. After he died, Rose continued to play tennis. She mostly plays with the men at the local club, and she's as good as any of them. June also said that she never dated any of those guys, or any other men for that matter. I don't know where June got her information, and I didn't ask. Rose also has a female tennis partner that she plays with regularly, and the rumor mill has it that her tennis partner is much more than just a tennis partner. So after June gives me all this information, she offers me her personal opinion, that Rose Peterson is physically unattractive. She is too muscular and too manly looking. You know, Stone, it's funny how women sometimes see certain things. I mean, in my opinion, Rose Peterson is very athletic looking, but she's definitely attractive and feminine. You know what I'm talking about, Stone?"

"Yes, Danny, I think I know exactly what you're talking about. Rose Peterson is a good looker, and most men would find her attractive. I think she's attractive too. She may also be gay. But regardless of her sexual preference, we both find her to be attractive, even though June, and probably some other women, think she's unattractive."

I continued, "You know, Danny, men and women are different."

Danny looked at me and smiled. "That's very perceptive, Stone. I'm happy you pointed that out. Thank God for that difference! I wouldn't have it any other way. Would you?"

"No, Danny, neither would I. But what I mean is that men and women think differently. They look at things differently, and they react to things differently. It's almost as though they were from different planets."

"Okay, Stone, it's a psychology thing. I get it. But what do we do now? We've got Salinas, Preston, and Peterson. Maybe one of them is the murderer, maybe none of them is. Should we lean on any of them? What's our next step?"

"I'm not sure, Danny. But I'm thinking, maybe it's time for another broker's open at Bedford House."

42

The more I thought about Big Howie, and the more I thought about Sam Salinas, Jr., Rose Peterson, and William Preston, the more clearly I remembered all three of them and the more convinced I became. It was time to flush out a murderer. It was time for a second Bedford House broker's open.

I had already mentioned to Ellen that I was thinking about having another broker's open at Bedford House. I had told her that if all of this was really over, the open house should go smoothly.

What I have not told her is that a number of suspects have surfaced since Big Howie's demise, and that this broker's open is a trap to catch a murderer. I don't want her to worry more—the less she knows, the safer she'll be.

I'll do this broker's open the same way as the ill-fated first broker's open. I'll send out the invitations and invite all the brokers just like before. It will be just like any other broker's open, especially now that there is nothing to worry about since the Bedford Murderer is no more. So nothing will be different for this open. Well, almost nothing. Maybe we'll plant some bugs there that weren't there before. Dannyboy can see to that, and he can listen from a distance, a far distance. He can make sure that there are no uninvited guests visiting Bedford House before the open. And he can keep an ear on things during the open as well. No, nothing different, except now it's February instead of December, and I am holding it open this time. If the murderer is still out there, what better bait to catch him with than the real thing, Stone the broker-realtor, Stone the Jew.

Nothing will be different, and everything will be different. Now it's a trap, with the best bait available—me. But it won't look like a trap. And it won't smell like a trap. The only two people who will know it is a trap will be Dannyboy and myself. There won't be any cover for me on this one. I'll take Dannyboy off my back. I can wear a bug, and he can listen from a distance. Maybe he can tape what goes on, if anything goes on. Everything about this broker's open must be natural.

There will be no police around. There will be no non-brokers or non-realtors around either. Just this big, beautiful house, some brokers and realtors, and maybe one murderer. Yes. One murderer. A madman who thinks that I shouldn't be in Duluth and that he can kill or do whatever he wants to get rid of me.

I will have the Beretta with me, of course. I can't forget about the beautiful Beretta. That small but powerful pistol was given to me as a gift, right after I made Detective. It's sleek and fits in my sport jacket pocket with no noticeable bulge. I've qualified with it many times before—even though it's not what I carried when I was on the force. I've maintained it meticulously. A bullet blasts out from its barrel with enough velocity and force to kill with one shot. One good shot. One less Bedford Murderer.

I will also have an advantage that the murderer won't have. I'll be expecting him and I'll be ready for him. He won't know that. Or she won't know that. I suppose the murderer could be a woman, but that is very unlikely. Based upon my past experience and police statistics, most brutal murders have been committed by men. So when he shows up at the broker's open, I have to be ready for him. And I will be.

43

The best thing that can happen from this second broker's open is that nothing can happen. I can be wrong and Detective June Brown and the Duluth Police Department can be right. The Bedford murder case is officially closed and it really is over. I'd like to believe that it's over, but I don't! For assurance and peace of mind, I have to do this broker's open again. Even if I was sure that it was over, I would still have to hold it open one more time. It's an important part of the marketing plan for selling Bedford House.

If the murderer is still out there, he will be invited to this second broker's open house in the same way that he was invited to the first one. If he hated me then, he'll hate me much more now. He told me to leave, not to sell here, or worse will happen. Well, I'm still here and I'm selling the biggest and the best listing of them all—the prestigious Bedford House.

What kind of rage and craziness will be exploding inside his head, this second time around? Will he try to kill me at Bedford House?

I can picture a terribly twisted psyche perfectly, but I can't see a person. I can see the shadow of a madman moving about, but I can't see a face. I can sense his intense anger, but I don't know why. I don't think his motive is real estate alone. It's got to be more than that, much more than that. But what? What is it that makes him hate me so much? Selling real estate may be just one part of it. Being Jewish another. But what is it that makes him snap? Maybe this second broker's open will make him go over the edge. Again!

Assuming that happens, the best case scenario would be to bring him in alive and see that he gets the justice he deserves. The second best case scenario would be to kill him before he kills me. In the back of my mind, and not too far back either, the second best case scenario keeps turning into the best case scenario. I keep thinking that this animal has no right to live. The worst case scenario is that he kills me. If that happens, Dannyboy can kill him.

I should just forget about these scenarios and kill the animal myself. It would be over then. But I don't think I could do that. That's the difference between animals and humans. God gave humans a conscience and the ability to know the difference between right and wrong. On the other hand, I'm not sure that killing him would be wrong. But I can't make that decision. Or can I?

44

I don't decide who lives or dies,
Not even when the proof there lies.
I cannot right poor victims' cries,
Not even when justice denies.

But I can hold this broker's open at Bedford House. And I can kill a murderer in self-defense. In most everybody's mind, it's just another open house. In my mind, it's a trap to catch a murderer, with me as both the bait and the trapper. In the murderer's mind, a perfect opportunity for "worse to happen," when no one is expecting anything to happen.

I can hear what this murderer is saying to himself. It's faint but clear, "What better time or place to rid Duluth of this Stone Jew." I can also hear my reply. It's loud and clear, "What better time or place to kill this murderer."

45

The Bedford House mansion sits on a two-acre lot, on a gently sloping hill overlooking Lake Superior. There is enough space to park in front of the house and some space at the side of the house as well. There's also an enormous carriage house in back of the house that's been partially converted to accommodate cars. No need to open that up today unless someone just has to see it. If you've seen one carriage house you've seen them all. Here's a picture and description of it. That should suffice.

If I stay by the window, it's easy to see the cars coming up the hill and parking by the house. I can also see the brokers and realtors getting out of their cars and walking up to the house. When I move away from the window I can see them as they enter the house, removing their heavy coats on this cold gray winter day. When they're ready to leave, I'll be able to watch them, as they get back into their cars and drive away. It's very easy arithmetic. Their cars come and their cars go. My car and his car stay. The trap will be set. But who will get trapped? We'll see. For now, I'd better tend to this bunch of brokers and realtors. I need to be a good host.

Everyone seems to be having a good time

checking out this house. I just need to mingle and smile, smile and mingle, talk and be natural. Natural, that's me today. As I look at them, I think to myself, what they wouldn't give or do to sell this house. Wait a second, that's not the right thought for now. In fact, it doesn't sound good at all. Imagine if all of these brokers or realtors were in on it. What would I do then? On the other hand, maybe June was right. Maybe it was Big Howie, and it's all over now. Okay, Stone, slow down and take it easy. Stop hallucinating. You know there's just one sicko here. Just one sicko, but who is it? Look at all these people. Okay, I just have to keep smiling. I have to keep hosting and watching. My internal radar was preset to Salinas, Peterson, and Preston. I haven't seen any of them yet, but I'll keep looking. The Beretta is still there. I reach inside my pocket and touch it. It feels good. I have to continue to stay alert and stay focused. And I have to continue to be natural. It's not easy to be natural when I'm feeling uneasy. What the hell am I doing here all alone with all these people?

It seems like I've been here for hours, but actually, only about an hour has passed. Some more people are arriving. Out of the corner of my eye, I see that one of them is Sam Salinas, Jr. My heart skips a beat and nearly jumps out of my chest. What do I do now? Stay calm. Keep smiling. Keep hosting. Should I try to keep an eye on him? No one is leaving. Some party this is turning out to be. So far, there are about seventeen people scattered about and looking around. There are some small groups here, some singles there. The rest could be anywhere, and I am only seeing about nine or ten of them. Okay, some people are starting to leave. They are saying good-bye to me and hope it sells fast. People are leaving; cars are turning around and going down the hill. I only have about one more hour to go. There are no new arrivals and some more people leaving. Cars are driving away. Cars are still out there. There are ten cars including mine. People are still wandering around inside the house. They could be anywhere.

I talk to two women. They tell me how much they love this house, with so many different rooms, incredible wood and stone everywhere. Such an elegant and enchanting house, like a castle from years past, but with today's updates and conveniences. One of them says, "Just imagine living in this house. What a house to list and sell." The other one says, "I dream about selling a house like this. It's a house to die for. Oh, no. I can't believe I said that. I'm sorry."

That got my attention—"a house to die for." The words flowed so freely from her lovely lips. How right she was. Someone did die for it. Would someone die for it again?

Okay, the two of them are leaving, and arranging to follow one another and go for lunch somewhere. I'm feeling spooked, and I'm thinking,

"Go to lunch, somewhere away from here," that sounds pretty good to me! Maybe I should get out of here while the getting is good.

They leave, I don't. I have to stay. Eight cars are still out there. Three more guys are talking and getting on their coats. I hear them talking about how cold and gray it is outside and about the snow that's slowly falling. One of them says, "It's a great house. What a listing to have. But after what happened here, I wonder if anyone will want to buy it." They leave. Three more gone. Three more cars sliding away. Slip, slip, slip, slide, slide, slide. Slip sliding away.

Very light snow has been falling for some time now. There are only five cars out there. Two other people leave simultaneously, so quickly that I miss their faces while I am getting an earful from a sophisticated lady in her late forties. I find her very sexy and seductive looking. "Okay, Stone, get a grip. Stay focused," I tell myself. She's telling me about a mansion that she sold when she was living in California. "It was an older couple getting divorced," she said. "Very nasty and at each other's throats—but nobody got killed." I'm listening to her at the same time that I'm doing the arithmetic in my head. There were five left before. Now two more hurry out, mumbling about the snow that's falling. Only three cars left—the sophisticated lady's, mine, and one other. I quickly look out the window while I'm listening. A black Lincoln is out there. Shit, it's Salinas's car.

BROKER'S OPEN

The snow is still slowly falling. It looks like a large white curtain covering the bare branches and cold leafless trees, and blanketing the ground with a plush new carpet of white. In the house are my lady here and Salinas somewhere. I'm feeling uneasy and I'm becoming unnerved. Shit, I'd feel better if Dannyboy was nearby. I've got to stay cool and confident. I have to smile, look natural, listen, talk, and take it easy. There's a song, something about a sophisticated lady. I can't remember its words, but I can hear Sinatra singing it inside my head. "Sophisticated lady stay," something like that. But this lady's not staying. She's smiling and asking for her coat. She sees it and says, "There it is." She adds, "You know, in an elegant house like this there should be a butler or manservant to help me on with my coat." I smile, grab the coat, and as she slips into it like a big cat, she gently and indiscreetly bumps and shimmies her derriere against my front, smiles at me, and says, "Thanks. Bye. Let's do it again sometime." She slips out to her car and she's gone.

I think about what she just said, "Let's do it again sometime." Do what? Bump, bump, shimmy, shimmy? I look out the window, and off she goes. Slip slip, slide slide. He's in the house. But where? Even if I knew, what would I do?

"I didn't want to interrupt you and Broker Stillman." The voice from behind startles me. I turn around slowly. I have to stay calm.

There he is, Sam Salinas, Jr., staring at me. "I didn't mean to sneak up on you like that," he says. "But I didn't want to come between the two of you. It looked like Broker Stillman was coming on to you a bit."

I looked at him, tried to relax, and replied, "I was just helping her on with her coat."

"How about that bump?" he asked. "And that shimmy?"

I looked at him and answered, "It was just an innocent bump. A harmless shimmy. Nothing to get excited about."

Salinas gave me a "yeah we know better" type of look.

As he continued looking at me, his eyes narrowed, and many small wrinkles appeared on his forehead. As he stared, I slowly curled my fingers around the pistol in my pocket.

"You know, Stone, I don't like your discounted commissions and your cash rebates. No, I don't like them at all."

This was what I was waiting for, as I replied, "Well that's too bad, because I like them, Salinas. I like them just fine."

He continued to watch me, as he reached into his suit jacket pocket.

My eyes were locked onto his arm and wrist as he slowly removed his hand. My arm, hand, and fingers were ready to move as one.

When his hand came out, he was holding a large key ring and set of car keys. He said, "The snow's falling faster now. I had better get going. It's a great house you've got here, Stone. A dying breed, these magnificent mansions." He smirked and added, "Good luck with it."

"Yeah, thanks," I replied.

He left and I was alone, my fingers glued to the pistol in my pocket, unable to loosen them. Finally, my brain ordered my hand to loosen its grip and let go. Reluctantly, my hand obeyed. I watched from the window, as the Lincoln slowly descended the snow-covered driveway. There were no cars out there except mine. They all came and they all left. A fine trap this turned out to be, but in my mind, and throughout the rest of my body, I felt relieved.

It was snowing harder now. I had better get going myself. I'd better start turning off the lights. I had a gut feeling about this case, and this house, and this broker's open. So I was wrong. It wouldn't be the first time. Or the last time either. But this time I'm happy I'm wrong. I'm thinking, it's better to be wrong and safe than to be right and unsafe. Does that make any sense? What am I thinking about? The case is closed. It's over. That's it. This open is also over. It's time to close up and go home.

I'll just gather up my stuff, the flyers and brochures in the living room, and get the heck out of here. On the other hand, maybe I'll just sit down for a while. What a great room and what a view of the lake. And what a lake it is. Ten percent of the world's fresh water right here in front of me. My mind begins to wander. Just minutes ago this house was bustling and alive with people. Now it is still and lonely. Beautiful but deserted and desolate. It's also unsettling and eerie. As I sit, I think, I wouldn't want to live here or be here by myself. What am I thinking? I am here by myself.

It wouldn't be lonely if Ellen was here. Ellen, Jane, and me. All living here together. The three of us could be very comfortable here. A house is just a house. Add people, add love, and it becomes a home. I've heard that saying so many times before, but it never rang as true, as loud, and as clear as it did now. I always feel good when I think about Ellen. I could sit here for hours, looking at the lake and thinking about Ellen. Okay, enough daydreaming. Time to get up. Time to get it together and get out of here. I'll go home, call Ellen, and see her tonight.

46

Happy and warm thoughts can stay with you for a while and make you feel good all over, but these thoughts did not hang around. They deserted me suddenly, banished by his voice and his sudden appearance. It was like he came from nowhere. And the words he spoke startled me and made my heart jump. *"So we're finally alone."* There was William Preston just seven or eight feet from me, with a pistol in his hand that was pointed at my chest. There was a sadistic smile on his face, more like a twisted smirk, but his voice was reserved and his words came to me very slowly.

"Yes, Stone, all the guests have gone. There's just the two of us."

I stared at him without moving a muscle. My heart was beating heavily against my chest, and my senses were heightened by a rush of adrenaline that made it difficult to stand still.

"And soon I'll do what I should have done three months ago, Stone." Now I could hear the hate in his voice and I could see the anger on his face.

He glared at me and continued speaking, "Same mansion, wrong realtor then. Right realtor now. Move over to that chair by the window and sit down with your hands on your lap. Don't think about trying anything or I'll kill you right now."

My brain told me to do exactly as I was told. The rest of my body told me to lunge at him and kill him. I wanted to reach for my gun and kill him, but I opted for the seat. It would make me a smaller target. It would also be easier for me to get a shot off.

"Listen, Stone, you'll die soon enough, but maybe you'd like to know why. Would you?"

In as calm a voice as I could manage, I said, "I would." I raised my left hand very slowly to scratch my nose, and he screamed to stop or he'd shoot. So I froze, and said very slowly that I was just going to scratch my nose.

"Well, scratch it, and put your hand back on your lap, and don't do it again, or I'll kill you right now. You understand?"

I said I did.

"It was all planned out perfectly, Stone. I would kill you during your broker's open. But I'd be vacationing in Hilton Head before, during, and after the broker's open. What a perfect alibi if I ever needed one. No one knew I flew back to Duluth. I used a false name and I paid cash for the ticket. I even flew back in a disguise. I wore size thirteen shoes, the same kind that Howard Simkey wore. What a pain to walk in those big stupid shoes. But I might as well lead the police in the direction of Big Howie. Yes, I knew how much he hated you. All of this just to be at your

BROKER'S OPEN

Bedford House broker's open. I got there well in advance of the open and waited. My plan was simple. I had a gun. This one. When you got there I'd kill you. Stone would be dead. I'd fly back to Hilton Head, still in disguise mind you, and finish my vacation. It was a perfect plan. But what happens, this pretty little bitch shows up instead of you. I was enraged. You let someone else do your broker's open for you. Typical of a scheming Jew. So I'm thinking that my plan is ruined. All my hard work was for nothing. Well, maybe not. It was time for a change of plans. I'd just kill the bitch instead. A brutal killing at that. That would teach you a lesson. It would be your fault that she was dead. Then you'd have to leave Duluth. But did you leave? No! You're still here!"

"I think I know the rest," I said. "But why? All this for real estate? That's crazy."

Preston was fuming. His eyes were full of hate and his voice became loud. "Real estate? You stupid Jew. You think you're so smart, don't you, Stone? But you have no idea what this is all about, do you? I could kill you right now, but I want you to know why before you die."

He continued to aim the gun at my chest and spoke deliberately, now in an arrogant voice. His words were chosen to humiliate and hurt me. There would be some serious suffering and pain before he'd kill me.

"Three things, Stone. First, you're in the same business that I'm in. You sell real estate, high-priced real estate, and I don't want you in my business. I'm fed up with your Jewish bullshit and gimmicks. All this talk about lower commission rates and cash rebates. I don't need to contend with this shit. Second, you're a goddamn no good Jew and you don't even belong here. I gave you a chance to leave, but no, you wouldn't take it. You'd rather see others die or suffer than leave. Typical of a Jew. Third and last, and much more important to me than the first two, you come back here and take Ellen away from me."

I couldn't believe what I was hearing. Why was this sick bastard talking about Ellen? I said, "I don't understand."

"Shut up!" he ordered. He waved the gun back and forth aiming at my chest, then my face, then my chest again. "That's right, Ellen. I got rid of her husband. It was easy enough. I ran him off the road and over the cliff. The police called it an accident. The newspapers said it was a terrible and tragic accident. With her husband gone, she'd soon be ready for me. Then you arrived, and you're with Ellen again. You don't know that I'm a client of hers." He smiled at me in a way that made me want to tear that grin right off his face, and then said, "There's nothing wrong with me; it was just a way for me to be close to her. I'd let her cure me. Ha! What a joke this psychology is. I'd be so thankful. I'd send her thank you notes, maybe even some flowers. I'd woo her slowly. I'd take her out and be with her. It would have just been a matter of time. And then you show up."

I couldn't listen to this anymore. I'll lunge at him now, that's the thing to do, all my adrenaline going strong, my muscles tensed, my brain and body on blast off. But I held back and stared at him and said, "Now I think I understand." As I gripped the small gun in my pocket, I said, "But what would make you think that a woman like Ellen would ever be intimately involved with a sick, crazy, ugly animal like you?" And as I said "like you," I lunged forward with one hand out and the Beretta firmly in the other. At the same time that he shot me in the chest, I think I shot him in the face or the neck or the head. I reeled backward as I heard a thundering explosion of glass, metal, and gunshot. Another shot. And another. There was a terrible pain in my chest. I fell down hard. And then nothing.

47

Some people believe and say that in death there is nonexistence. In death there is no more and no less. There is nothing. But no one knows what death is like except the dead. That very moment when life ends and death begins is the first time one knows what death is like. And I know what death is like. Yes, I know the truth of death. I lie suspended with no feeling and no movement. No happiness, no sadness, and no pain. Nothing at all. No sight, no hearing, no smell, no taste, and no touch. There's nothing but a kind of electric force that comes and goes—intangible thought waves attached to a soul without a body. There's no light, yet there's no darkness. But if this is so, what are these very faint oval lights that seem to be dancing in the distance in front of me? Sometimes they seem to brighten and then dim. These oval shapes of light are changing in front of me. They're getting brighter, and clearer, and closer. They're ovals within oval lights. They're fuzzy on the top. They're wet in the middle. They're happy at the bottom. They're faces. Faces of Ellen, Jane, and Dannyboy. They're crying and smiling at the same time. What are they doing here? They should be alive.

48

The Dannyboy face was the first to speak. "Well, it's about time. Just nod your head if you know who I am."

I nodded my head. I was able to nod my head.

"Okay, Stone, you've been unconscious for two days. You've been in a coma, dead to the world. Don't try to talk. I know that look of yours. Just listen, and I'll tell you what happened."

Dannyboy could be a tough guy when he had to be. But today he wasn't tough. He wiped his wet eyes and continued to speak, "Here's how it went down. Your bulletproof vest saved your life, but it's an older model vest, and you could have been killed. You took a direct hit in the chest, and there was some penetration and a lot of impact— even with the vest. Not enough to kill you, but enough to hurt you. Enough to send you falling backward with so much force that when you fell, you banged your head hard enough to make you unconscious."

Danny paused and smiled, "Even with a head as hard as yours. Anyway, there I am in the living room, hiding in that colossal smoked glass entertainment center, staying as quiet and as still as I can. I can hear and I can see out. No one can see in. I was just about to take him out, when you did your superman lunge at him. I came smashing out of that glass, and shot William Preston at the same time or a split second after he shot you. And you shot him. Your shot hit him in the head. Probably fatal. I squeezed off two more to make sure. There was smashed broken glass everywhere. What a mess!"

I looked at Dannyboy and smiled. I had never thought I'd see him again. I know the truth of death. William Preston of Preston Properties is dead. Larry Stone is alive. Dannyboy moved closer to me. He gently touched my shoulder, leaned down very close to my face, and said, "God, I'm happy you're back, Stone. I'll see you later." And then he was gone.

49

Ellen, with happy tears in her eyes, laughing and crying at the same time, held my hand. She moved her face close to mine, so close that her teardrops gently wet my eyes, as her lips touched mine in a sweet and tender kiss. Her daughter, Jane, held my other hand, tightly for an eight-year-old, and gently brushed her cheek against mine.

I looked at both of them, and felt the strength of love inside me. Happiness like a gentle river running through the land flowed throughout my body. It brought me to a peaceful place in time, and for a moment, I saw the faces of my parents smiling at me lovingly. I knew that I was with family once more.

Ellen kissed me again, and life stirred inside me. She said, "I love you, Larry."

Jane said, "I love you, too."

With renewed strength and thankfulness, I put one arm around Ellen and the other around Jane. I smiled and said, "I love you both."

I looked at Ellen and very slowly said, "By the way, Ellen, no more broker's opens at Bedford House for me. Maybe I should just buy the place. What do you think about us getting married, settling down, and living at Bedford House?"

Ellen looked at me lovingly, a smile on her face and a gleam in her eyes. She said, "Yes, no, and maybe."